This Bible belongs to

_____

Received on _____

Passed on to

_____

_____

_____

_____

_____

_____

JPS
Illustrated
Children's Bible

JPS
Illustrated
Children's Bible

—•❋•—

Retold by Ellen Frankel

Illustrated by Avi Katz

2009 • 5769
The Jewish Publication Society
Philadelphia

JPS is a nonprofit educational association and the oldest and foremost publisher of Judaica in English in North America. The mission of JPS is to enhance Jewish culture by promoting the dissemination of religious and secular works, in the United States and abroad, to all individuals and institutions interested in past and contemporary Jewish life.

The Jewish Publication Society
2100 Arch Street, 2nd floor
Philadelphia, PA 19103
www.jewishpub.org

Design and Composition by Alexa Ginsburg

Printed in China

09 10 11 12 10 9 8 7 6 5 4 3 2 1

ISBN: 978-0-8276-0891-7

Library of Congress Cataloging-in-Publication Data:

Frankel, Ellen.
    JPS illustrated children's Bible / Ellen Frankel ; illustrated by Avi Katz.—1st edition.
       p. cm.
    ISBN 978-0-8276-0891-7
    1. Bible stories, English—O.T. I. Katz, Avi. II. Title. III. Title: Jewish Publication Society illustrated children's Bible.
    BS551.2.F665 2009
    221.9'505--dc22

                              2008043163

JPS books are available at discounts for bulk purchases for reading groups, special sales, and fundraising purchases. Custom editions, including personalized covers, can be created in larger quantities for special needs. For more information, please contact us at marketing@jewishpub.org or at this address: 2100 Arch Street, Philadelphia, PA 19103.

To Riley Hannah and Teagan Rebecca,

חנה ריינצ ואליה תמר

To whom I bequeath the treasures contained in this book.

Cherish them and teach them to your children.

Contents

Introduction

Once upon a time...

As soon as we read these words, we know that we are leaving our workaday world to enter a land of make-believe, where wishes make things so and where ever after is always happy. As children, we gladly gave ourselves up to this dream, but we have since lost our innocence, and so we read on, charmed but not taken in.

It's different with the Bible. It doesn't begin with "Once upon a time." Instead, the first sentence steps forward onto hard bedrock: "When God began to create heaven and earth." This is not the world of make-believe. But neither is it the world we ordinarily inhabit. It's the liminal realm of prehistory, of God's reality, the moment before the Big Bang. The stories in the Bible defy the neat conventions of fairy tales: many a hero lives unhappily ever after, and many maidens remain in distress. These stories are linked together in a chain of consequences: the sins of the fathers are visited upon a hundred generations; villainy dooms whole nations; an act of faith summons angels. No wonder this Book of Books has endured for two millennia.

How then does one take this often disturbing account of the Jewish national story and make it suitable for children?

Over the centuries, many have made the attempt, mostly in the Christian community. In the 12th century, French writer Peter Comestor produced a popular illustrated children's Bible in Latin, *Historia Scholastica,* intended for Christian children and uneducated adults. A few centuries later, the invention of the printing press resulted in the mass production of children's Bibles, most notably, Martin Luther's children's Bible, an abridged illustrated version of his German Bible translation. For the most part, these Bibles were intended for moral instruction; their authors pressed the Bible into service for this aim. Thus biblical stories were expurgated, abridged, rewritten, and more often than not, Christianized. The Bible was thus turned into a morality play for children.

The Jewish community has also long used the Bible for the moral instruction of its children, but it has done so not by rewriting the original text as in Christian children's Bibles but by filtering it through the interpretations and fables of the rabbinic sages. Jewish tradition has always regarded the Hebrew Bible as the foundation of its "core curriculum" of lifelong learning. That is why, according to the popular anthology of early rabbinic teachings known as Pirke Avot (Ethics of the Fathers), a child's education should begin at age five with Bible study. An important part of this core Bible curriculum are the interpretations by the classical Rabbis, who refract the Bible through the dual prism of exegesis, or *peshat* (reading out of the text on its own terms) and eisegesis, or *derash* (reading into the text from the perspective of one's own time and place). In effect, then, though Jewish children begin their education with the Hebrew Bible, it is really the Rabbis' Bible that they study—the Hebrew text as interpreted—and reimagined by—the ancient sages.

In modern times, especially in the United States, Jews have adapted this traditional core curriculum to suit American need and tastes. Early on, many Jewish teachers and textbook publishers borrowed from the theories and practices of American educational philosophers, especially John Dewey. What has emerged over time is a new kind of specialized Jewish children's literature, including Bible stories written and illustrated expressly to further the moral and intellectual development of young readers.

Unfortunately, the Bible does not sit comfortably within the framework of Western liberal education. More often than not, biblical explanations about the how's and why's of nature clash with the theories of modern science. The tribal politics of ancient Israel may offend some modern sensibilities. And some parts of the Bible are too violent, sexually explicit, or culturally alien for today's children. So, like their Christian counterparts, Jewish children's Bibles have generally represented ingenious compromises. Through abridgment, censorship, euphemism, and tact, the authors of these Bibles have cut scripture down to scale, sometimes preserving the essence of the original, other times making a hash of it.

The same is true of the illustrations that usually appear in these American editions. Pictorial styles range from realism to cartoons, from photographic precision to Disney fantasy. Although pictures in modern children's Bibles do not generally allegorize their subjects as was the case in earlier centuries, artists cannot neutrally depict a biblical scene. Like rabbinic commentaries, landscapes and figures necessarily reflect what the illustrator reads into and out of the biblical text. Indeed, all translation, even from word into image, is interpretation.

This Jewish children's Bible is different from others.

My principal aim in this volume is to reproduce the unique texture and rhythm of biblical language, specifically, that of the 1985 JPS English Translation (NJPS), which itself aims to capture the idiomatic nuances of biblical Hebrew. The stories that you find within these pages are abridged but not improved or modernized. Whenever possible, I have kept the NJPS wording, so that my readers and listeners can appreciate the simple narrative style of the Bible: sentences anchored in active subjects and verbs, few adjectives or adverbs, only rare editorializing by the narrator. Like any good yarn, much of every Bible story is told through dialogue, with "He said" or "She said" inserted only to differentiate speakers. All the familiar techniques of good storytelling—suspense, dramatic irony, repetition, wordplay, stock characters—are present in these stories, but the specific ways that these techniques play out are unique to the Hebrew Bible. So, too, are the names of people and places, of holy days and sacred acts.

I have selected 53 stories for inclusion in this book. My choices were guided mainly by my sense of what makes a good story for children, but a few were included because they are pivotal to an understanding of the Jewish national story. Some I excluded as being inappropriate for young readers. Much more was left out than left in: poetry, prophecy, songs, psalms, genealogies, legal material, ritual and priestly material, wisdom literature, and folklore. I leave this for others to translate for children.

As I worked, I made many judgment calls—about word choice, translation, editorial intervention, censorship, and gendered language. In the back of this volume, in a special section called "Writing a Jewish Children's Bible: An Author's Notebook," you can find brief explanations about my editorial choices, with a few examples to illustrate them. These notes are intended for teachers, rabbis, librarians, and parents who want to understand in greater detail how my version compares to NJPS.

Rabbi Ben Bag Bag, one of the sages of the Mishnah, said of the Torah: "Turn it and turn it, for everything is in it." Although the volume in your hands does not contain the whole Torah, it's a good first leg of your journey toward Ben Bag Bag's promised reward. I pray that you find wisdom, inspiration, and delight along the way.

Ellen Frankel
25 Tammuz 5768
July 28, 2008

JPS
Illustrated
Children's Bible

The Creation of the World

Genesis 1:1–2:4

In the very beginning, God created a world—the heavens and the earth—out of nothing. But this world was without rhyme or reason. Darkness covered the face of the deep, and the breath of God glided over the waters.

Then God said, "Let there be light!"

And there was light.

God saw that the light was good.

Then God separated the light from the darkness. God called the light Day, and the darkness Night.

And there was evening and there was morning: a first day.

Then God said, "Let a great space open up between the waters, separating them." God created this great space, separating the waters above from the waters below. God called this great space Sky.

And there was evening and there was morning: a second day.

Then God said, "Let the waters below the sky come together into one place, so dry land can appear." And so it happened. God called the dry land Earth, and the coming together of the waters, God called Oceans.

And God saw that this was good.

Then God said, "Let the earth give birth to green growing things—plants bearing seeds, and trees bearing fruit."

And God saw that this was good. And there was evening and there was morning: a third day.

Then God said, "Let lights appear in the sky to separate day from night. They will tell time in days and years."

And so it happened.

Then God made the two great lights: the bigger light—the Sun—to rule the day, and the smaller light—the Moon—to rule the night; and the stars.

And God saw that this was good.

And there was evening and there was morning: a fourth day.

Then God said, "Let the waters overflow with life, and let flying creatures soar above the earth across the open sky."

Then God created the great sea monsters, and every kind of living thing that swims and flies. And God saw that this was good.

God blessed them all and said, "Fill the oceans and the sky!"

And there was evening and there was morning: a fifth day.

Then God said, "Let every kind of living creature arise upon the earth— tame animals and creeping things and wild beasts."

And so it happened.

God made every kind of tame animal and creeping thing and wild animal.

And God saw that this was good.

Then God said, "Let's create a human being who takes after us. This being will rule the fish of the sea, the birds of the sky, the tame animals, all the creeping things, and the whole earth."

So God created a human being, both male and female—*Adam*—made in God's image.

God blessed them and said to them, "Be fruitful and multiply, fill the earth and tame it, and rule over the fish of the sea, the birds of the sky, and all living things that creep on the earth. I give to you as food all the seed-bearing plants and fruit trees. And I also give the plants as food to all the

animals on the land, the birds in the sky, everything that creeps and breathes on the earth."

   And God looked at all of creation and found it very good.

   And there was evening and there was morning: the sixth day.

   On the seventh day, the heavens and earth were finished, and God rested. God blessed the seventh day and called it holy, because on that day God rested from all the work of creating.

Adam and Eve

Genesis 2:5–2:24

When God made the earth and the heavens, no bushes grew, no grasses sprouted in the fields, because God had not yet sent rain to the earth, and there was no one to work the soil. A mist rose up from the ground and watered the face of the earth.

Then God formed a man, Adam, from the dust of the earth, and blew the breath of life into his nostrils, and Adam came to life.

Then God planted a garden in Eden and put the new-made man there to take care of it. God made trees grow from the ground, every kind of tree that was lovely to look at and good to eat. And in the middle of the garden grew the Tree of Life and the Tree of Knowing Good and Evil.

God commanded Adam: "You may eat from every tree in the garden—except from the Tree of Knowing Good and Evil. For if you were to eat from that tree, you would surely die."

Then God said, "It is not good for Adam to be alone. I will make a proper partner for him."

So God shaped out of earth all the wild animals and the birds and brought them to Adam to name them. Adam gave names to all the field animals and the birds of the sky and all the wild beasts. But Adam still had no proper partner.

Then God put Adam to sleep, and while he was sleeping, took a rib out of his side and closed up the skin there. God shaped the rib into a woman and brought her to Adam.

Adam said, "This one at last is bone of my bones and flesh of my flesh. She will be called woman, *eesha*, because out of man, *eesh*, she was taken."

The Serpent in the Garden

Genesis 3

The man and the woman were both naked, but they did not feel ashamed.

Then the serpent, the trickiest of all the wild animals, said to the woman, "Did God really say, 'You can't eat from *any* of the trees in the garden'?"

The woman answered, "We may eat fruit from all of the trees — except the one that grows in the middle of the garden. God told us, 'Do not eat from that tree, because if you do, you could die.'"

"You are not going to die!" said the serpent. "God knows that as soon as you eat fruit from that tree, your eyes will be opened and you will be just like God, who understands good and evil."

When the woman saw how delicious the fruit looked and how lovely it was to look at, and when she imagined how wise it would make her, she took some of the fruit and ate it. Then she gave some to her husband, and he ate it, too.

Suddenly their eyes were opened. They realized that they were naked, so they sewed fig leaves together and covered themselves. No sooner had they done so than they heard the voice of God gliding through the garden. Quickly they hid from God among the trees.

God called out to Adam, "Where are you?"

Adam replied, "I heard your voice in the garden, and I was afraid because I was naked, so I hid."

"Who told you that you were naked?" asked God. "Did you eat from the forbidden tree?"

"The woman you put beside me—she gave me fruit from that tree, and I ate it."

"What have you done?" God asked the woman.

She replied, "The serpent tricked me, so I ate the fruit."

God said to the serpent, "Because you did this, you will be the most cursed of all beasts! You will crawl on your belly and eat dirt all the days of your life. You and the woman will hate each other, and her children will hate your children. They will strike at your head, and you will strike at their heel."

To the woman God said, "I will make it painful for you to have children. But you will still want your husband, who will rule over you."

And to Adam God said, "Because you did as your wife said and ate from the forbidden tree, the ground will be cursed because of you. It will sprout thorns and thistles; and you will have to work hard to make it produce food. By the sweat of your brow you will earn your bread, until you return to the ground from which you were taken. For you are only dust, and to dust you will return."

Adam gave his wife the name Eve, Hava, because she was the mother of life, *hayim*.

God then made for Adam and Eve clothing out of animal skin, and covered them.

Then God said, "Now that human beings have become like us,

understanding good and evil, what if they should eat fruit from the Tree of Life and live forever?"

So God drove Adam and Eve out of the Garden of Eden, so that they would have to live off the soil from which they came. Then God stationed winged cherubim and a fiery, ever-spinning sword at the gates of Eden, to block the way back to the Tree of Life.

The First Murder

Genesis 4:1–16

Adam's wife, Eve, became pregnant and gave birth to Cain. Then she gave birth to his brother, Abel.

Abel became a shepherd, and Cain became a farmer.

Cain offered God a gift from his harvest. Abel offered God the best of his flock. God accepted Abel's offering, but paid no attention to Cain's.

And Cain was very angry.

"Why are you so angry?" God asked Cain. "If you do what is right, you will be accepted. If you do not, sin lies in wait for you—but you can master it!"

Later, when they were together in the field, Cain attacked his brother, Abel, and killed him.

God asked Cain, "Where is your brother, Abel?"

Cain replied, "I do not know. Am I my brother's keeper?"

God said to him, "What have you done? Your brother's blood cries out to Me from the ground! Now you will be even more cursed than the ground. When you work the soil, it will no longer produce for you. You will become a homeless wanderer on the earth."

Cain cried, "My punishment is too hard for me! Now that You have driven me away from You, anyone who meets me will kill me."

So God put a mark on Cain to protect him from anyone who might want to kill him.

Then Cain left God's presence and settled in the land of Nod, east of Eden.

The Great Flood

Genesis 6:9–9:29

When God saw how wicked people on earth had become, God was sorry about creating human beings.

God said, "I will wipe them out, together with all the animals, creeping things, and birds, for I am sorry that I made them."

But Noah found favor in God's eyes.

This is the story of Noah's family. Noah was a decent man, righteous in his own time. Noah had three sons: Shem, Ham, and Japhet.

By now the earth had become violent and wild. When God saw how spoiled the earth was, God said to Noah, "I have decided to put an end to all living things on earth. The earth is filled with violence because of them, so I am going to destroy them with the earth."

God told Noah, "Make yourself a giant wooden ark, covered inside and outside with tar. Make a window in the roof to let the daylight in, and a door in the side. Make three decks on the inside."

And God said, "I am about to bring a flood upon the earth to destroy all living things. Everything on earth will die.

"But I will make a covenant with you, the only righteous person I have found in this generation. You will come into the ark with your sons and your wife, and your sons' wives. Bring into the ark at least one pair of every kind of living thing—birds, animals, and creeping things—to keep them alive together with you and your family. Bring seven pairs of every permitted animal, male and female, and one pair of every forbidden animal, to keep their kind alive on the earth. Take some of everything edible and store it away, as food for you and for them."

Noah did just as God commanded him.

Then God told Noah, "Go into the ark with your whole family. In seven days I will bring rain upon the earth, for 40 days and 40 nights, and I will wipe out all life that I have created."

And Noah did just as God commanded him.

Noah was 600 years old when the Flood came. He went into the ark with his sons, his wife, his sons' wives, permitted animals and forbidden ones, with birds and every creature that creeps on the ground. They came to Noah two by two, a male and a female, as God had commanded. On that same day, Noah, his family, and all the animals went into the ark, at least two of every living thing that breathes air. Then God shut Noah in.

And on the seventh day the waters of the Flood rained down upon the earth.

In the second month of the year, on the 17th day of the month, all the underground fountains burst, and the windows of the sky broke open.

The Flood continued for 40 days. The waters swelled and raised the ark above the earth, so that it floated on top of the waters. Then the waters rose even higher, covering the tallest mountains and then rising above them. And everything that breathed the breath of life—people, tame and wild animals, creeping things, and birds of the sky—all were wiped out.

Only Noah and those with him in the ark remained alive.

Then, after 150 days, God remembered Noah and all who were with him in the ark. God sent a wind to blow across the earth, and it sealed up the

fountains underground and the windows of the sky. Then the rain was held back. And the waters began to recede.

In the seventh month, on the 17th day of the month, the ark came to rest on the mountains of Ararat. The waters kept going down until the 10th month. On the first day of that month, the mountaintops reappeared.

At the end of 40 days, Noah opened the window of the ark and sent out a raven, which flew back and forth until the waters dried up from the earth.

Then he sent out a dove to see whether the waters had gone down. But the dove could not find a resting place, so she returned to the ark, and Noah took her in.

He waited another seven days and sent the dove out again. This time when the dove returned toward evening, she held in her beak a fresh-plucked olive leaf. Then Noah knew that the waters had gone down. He waited another seven days and sent out the dove again. This time she did not come back.

In his six hundred and first year, in the first month, on the first day of the month, Noah removed the ark's covering and saw that the earth was drying out. Two months later, the earth was dry.

God then said to Noah, "Come out of the ark, you and your family. Bring out with you all the living things inside the ark—birds, animals, and everything that creeps on earth—and let them spread over the earth and multiply."

So Noah came out with his family. And all the animals came out by families.

Then Noah built an altar and gave thanks to God.

God was pleased with Noah's offerings, and thought, "Never again will I doom the earth because people sin. Nor will I ever again destroy every living thing as I have just done. So long as the earth survives, these are the things that will never end: planting time and harvest, cold and heat, summer and winter, day and night."

God blessed Noah and his children and said to them, "Multiply and fill the earth. I turn over to you all the beasts of the earth, the birds of the sky, and the fish of the sea. Every creature that lives and everything that grows from the earth will be yours to eat. But you must not eat meat with blood still in it. And I will hold you responsible if you shed blood. For human beings were made in God's image."

God said to Noah and his children, "I'm now making a covenant with you and your descendants, and with every living thing on earth—birds, tame animals, and all wild beasts. I promise that never again will all life be cut off by the waters of a flood, and never again will a flood destroy the earth.

"This is the sign of the covenant between Me and you, and every living creature on earth, for all time. I have set My rainbow in the clouds, and it will be a sign of My promise to the earth. When I bring clouds over the earth, and the rainbow appears in the clouds, I will remember My promise to all living creatures: that the earth's waters will never again become a flood to destroy all life."

The Tower of Babel

Genesis 11:1–9

In those days, everyone on earth spoke the same language. And they settled in a valley in the land of Shinar.

They said to one another, "Come, let us make bricks and bake them hard. Let us build a city here, with a tower reaching up into the sky, so that we can make a name for ourselves. Otherwise, we will be scattered all over the world."

Then God came down to look at this city and this tower that human beings had built.

"If they have begun to act this way because they all speak the same language," God said, "then there is nothing to stop them from doing whatever they want. I will go down and mix up their speech, so that they will not be able to understand each other."

So God mixed up their language and they stopped building their city. And God scattered them across the face of the earth. That is why the place is called Babel, because there God babbled human speech.

Abram and Sarai Leave Home

Genesis 12:1–8

When Abram was 75 years old, God said to him, "Leave the land where you were born, and your parents' house, and go to the land that I will show you. I will make you into a great nation, and bless you, and make you famous. I will bless everyone who blesses you, and curse everyone who curses you. And all the families on earth will bless themselves in your name."

So Abram left his home as God had commanded him. With him were his wife, Sarai, and his nephew Lot. They brought with them all their wealth and the people they had gathered together, and headed for the land of Canaan. When they arrived there, God said to Abram, "I will give this land to your children and your grandchildren and all who come after them."

Then Abram built an altar and gave thanks to God.

The Birth of Ishmael

Genesis 16–17:5

Sarai and Abram grew very old. They still had no children, even though God had promised Abram that he would be the father of many nations.

One day Sarai said to her husband, "Take my Egyptian maid, Hagar. Maybe she will give you a son."

Abram listened to Sarai and took her maid, Hagar, as a wife. But when Hagar became pregnant, she began to look down on her mistress, Sarai.

Sarai said to Abram, "This is your fault! I gave you Hagar. Now she looks down on me because she is pregnant with your child. Let God decide whose side to take—yours or mine!"

Abram said, "Your maid is in your hands. Do whatever you think is right."

Sarai treated Hagar harshly, and Hagar ran away.

An angel of God found Hagar alongside a spring of water in the wilderness, and said to her, "Hagar, slave of Sarai, where have you come from, and where are you going?"

Hagar replied, "I am running away from my mistress, Sarai."

The angel said, "Go back to your mistress, and accept her harsh treatment." The angel continued, "You will be blessed with many children,

too many to count. You are about to have a son, and you will call him Ishmael, which means "God listens," for God has listened to your suffering. Your son will be a wild man, his fists always raised up."

Then Hagar gave God a new name, El-ro'i, "God of Seeing," for she said, "I have gone on seeing even after God has seen me!'"

Hagar returned to the camp and gave birth to a son, whom Abram named Ishmael.

Some time later, God gave Abram a new name, Abraham, which means "the father of many nations." God also gave Sarai a new name, Sarah, which means "princess."

Sarah Laughs

Genesis 18:1–15

One day three men came to visit Abraham and Sarah in their tent. As soon as Abraham saw them, he invited them to rest under a nearby oak tree and to eat and drink before traveling on their way. Abraham chose a calf from his herd and ordered his servants to cook it, and Sarah ran to make them cakes of fine flour.

One of the strangers said to Abraham, "I will come back next year, and your wife, Sarah, will give birth to a son!"

Sarah was listening from inside the tent, and she laughed when she heard the man's words.

"I have never had any children," she thought, "and I am now too old to have any. I am 90 years old, and Abraham is almost 100!"

God said to Abraham, "Why did Sarah laugh? Is anything too amazing for God? I will come back next year at this time, and Sarah will have a son."

Sarah was too frightened to tell God the truth so she lied, saying, "I did not laugh!"

God said to her, "But you did laugh."

Sodom and Gomorrah

Genesis 18:16–19:38

Then the three strangers went walking with Abraham, and they headed toward Sodom.

God thought, "I have singled out Abraham to teach his children what is right. Should I not tell him what I am about to do?"

So God said to Abraham, "The sins of Sodom and Gomorrah are very great! I will go down to see if what I have heard about them is true. If it is not, I will reconsider what I am about to do."

Then two of the men—who were in fact angels—continued on their way down to Sodom. Abraham remained talking with God.

Abraham said, "Will you destroy those who are righteous along with the guilty? What if there are 50 righteous people in Sodom—will you destroy them, too? Will you not forgive the town for the sake of the 50 righteous people who live there? Should not the Judge of the World act justly?"

God answered, "If I find 50 righteous people there, I will forgive the town because of them."

Abraham said, "What if the righteous fall five short? Will you destroy the whole town because five are missing?"

God answered, "I will not destroy it if I find 45."

"What if only 40 can be found?"

God answered, "For the sake of 40, I will not do it."

Abraham said, "Do not be angry, my Lord, if I ask for the sake of 30."

God said, "Very well, for the sake of 30."

"And what if only 20 can be found?" asked Abraham.

"I will not destroy it," God answered, "for the sake of 20."

Abraham said, "I will speak one last time, my Lord. Please do not be angry. What if only 10 are found?"

God answered, "I will not destroy it even for the sake of ten."

Then God stopped speaking, and Abraham returned to his tent.

The two angels came to Sodom in the evening, and met Abraham's nephew Lot at the town gate. Lot said to them, "Please spend the night in my house. Then early tomorrow, you can go on your way."

"No," they said, "we will spend the night in the town square."

But Lot pleaded with them to stay with him. So they came to his house, where he served them a feast.

Before Lot's guests went to sleep, all the men of Sodom, young and old, surrounded Lot's house and shouted, "Where are those men who came to you tonight? Bring them out so we can have some fun with them!"

Lot came out and shut the door behind him. He said, "Please, my friends, do not do them any harm. Look, I have two unmarried daughters. Do whatever you want with them, only do not harm my guests who have asked for shelter under my roof."

But the men said, "Get out of our way! We will deal worse with you than with them!"

They pushed forward to break down the door. But the angels pulled Lot back into the house and shut the door. Then they blinded the people outside with blazing light so they could not find the door.

The angels said to Lot, "Take your family away from this place. We are about to destroy the town because of its great evil."

Lot told his sons-in-law, "We must leave this place, because God is about to destroy it."

But they thought he was only joking, and they would not leave.

At sunrise, the angels told Lot: "Flee with your wife and your two daughters, or you will be swept away along with this evil town."

Lot hesitated, so the angels grabbed his hands and the hands of his wife and daughters, and led them away from the town.

The angels said to them, "Run for your lives! But do not look back, and do not stop anywhere on the plain."

As the sun came up, God rained down fire from heaven on Sodom and Gomorrah. God destroyed all the cities of the plain and everything that grew around them.

Lot's wife looked back and turned into a pillar of salt.

The next morning, when Abraham looked down upon the plain and saw smoke rising from the ground, he knew that God had destroyed Sodom and Gomorrah. But out of respect for Abraham, God had spared his nephew Lot.

The Birth of Isaac

Genesis 21:1–21

God remembered the promise to Sarah. Although she was 90 years old, Sarah now gave birth to a son at the time God had set. Abraham called his newborn son Isaac, *Yitzhak*, meaning "he will laugh."

Sarah said, "God has indeed given me laughter. Everyone who hears about this will laugh with me!"

When Isaac was eight days old, Abraham circumcised him, as God had commanded. Abraham was 100 years old when Isaac was born.

One day Sarah saw Hagar's son, Ishmael, clowning around.

She said to Abraham, "Send away that slave-woman and her son. My son will not share his inheritance with the son of a slave!"

Abraham was very upset, but God said to him, "Do not be upset about the boy or his mother. Do whatever Sarah tells you, for it is through Isaac that your line will continue. As for your other son, I will also make him into a nation, since he too is your son."

Early the next morning, Abraham took some bread and a waterskin, put them on Hagar's shoulder along with her child, and sent them away into the desert.

When the water was gone, Hagar placed Ishmael under a bush and sat down a bowshot away, thinking, "I do not want to watch my child die." Then she burst into tears.

God heard the boy crying, and an angel called out to Hagar, "Do not be afraid. God has heard the boy crying where he is. God will make him into a great nation."

Then God opened her eyes and she saw a well. She filled the skin with water and gave it to her son.

God was with Ishmael as he grew up. Ishmael lived in the wilderness and became an archer. And his mother found a wife for him from the land of Egypt.

The Binding of Isaac

Genesis 22:1–19

Some time later, God tested Abraham.

God said, "Abraham!"

Abraham answered, "Here I am."

God said, "Take your son, your only son, the one you love, Isaac, and go to the land of Moriah. There you will sacrifice him upon the mountain that I will point out to you."

Early the next morning, Abraham saddled his donkey and took with him two servants and his son, Isaac. He split the wood for the sacrifice, and headed toward the place that God had named.

On the third day Abraham looked up and saw the mountain in the distance.

Abraham said to his servants, "Stay here with the donkey. The boy and I will go up on the mountain. We will pray there and then return to you."

Abraham took the wood for the sacrifice and strapped it to his son, Isaac. In his own hand he took the firestone and the knife, and the two of them walked off together.

Isaac said to Abraham, "Father."

Abraham answered, "Here I am, my son."

"Here are the firestone and the wood, but where is the sheep for the sacrifice?"

Abraham replied, "God will provide the sheep for the sacrifice, my son."

Then the two of them walked on together.

They came to the place God had told Abraham about. There Abraham built an altar and arranged the wood on it. Then he bound up his son, Isaac, and laid him on the altar on top of the wood.

Then Abraham raised the knife to kill his son.

But an angel of God called out to him from heaven, "Abraham! Abraham!"

Abraham answered, "Here I am."

The angel said, "Do not raise your hand against the boy or do anything to hurt him, because now I know that you honor and fear God, since you have not held back from Me even your own son, your only son."

Abraham looked up and saw a ram caught by its horns in a thornbush. And Abraham sacrificed the ram instead of his son.

Then the angel of God called to Abraham from heaven a second time: "Because you did not hold back your only son, I will give you My blessing, and make your children as countless as the stars of the heavens and the sands of the shore. Your descendants will defeat their enemies. All the nations of the earth will bless themselves by your descendants, because you have listened to My voice."

Then Abraham went back to his servants, and together they returned home.

Rebekah at the Well

Genesis 23:1–2; 24

Sarah died at the age of 127, and Abraham mourned her.

Abraham was now old, blessed by God in all things.

And Abraham called the servant who ran his household, and said to him, "Swear by the God of heaven and earth that you will not take a wife for my son Isaac from among the Canaanite women but will go back to the land of my birth to find a wife for him."

The servant said, "But what if the woman I find there refuses to come with me? Should I take your son back there to marry her?"

"No, you must not take him back there. God will send an angel before you, and you will find a wife there for my son. And if the woman does not agree to follow you, then you are no longer bound by your promise to me. But do not take my son back there."

The servant swore to do what Abraham had asked.

The servant then set out with ten camels and many gifts and traveled back to the place where Abraham's brother Nahor lived.

He arrived at the well outside the town at evening, when the women came to draw water. The servant made his camels kneel down by the well, and he prayed, "God of my master Abraham, grant me good luck today and be kind to my master Abraham. When the young women come here, give me a sign. The young woman to whom I say—'Please lower your jar so that I may drink,' if she answers—'Drink, and I will also water your camels'—let her be the one You have chosen for Isaac."

As soon as he was done speaking, Rebekah—the granddaughter of Abraham's brother Nahor—came to the well. She was very beautiful and not yet married. She filled her jar with water and placed the jar on her shoulder to carry it. Abraham's servant ran up to her and asked her for water.

She lowered her jar, and said, "Drink, my lord."

When he had finishing drinking from her jar, she said to him, "Let me also draw water for your camels."

She returned to the well, drew more water, and emptied the water into the trough for all the camels.

The servant gave the young woman a gold nose-ring and two golden bracelets, and asked her, "Whose daughter are you? Is there room tonight for us in your father's house?"

She replied, "I am Rebekah, Bethuel's daughter, the granddaughter of Milcah and Nahor. We have plenty of straw and feed for your camels and room for you."

The servant bowed before God and offered a prayer: "Blessed be God, who has guided me on my errand, leading me to the house of my master's family."

Rebekah ran ahead and told her family all that had happened. When Rebekah's brother, Laban, saw the gold jewelry his sister was wearing, he went to the well and said to Abraham's servant, who was still there with his camels, "Why are you still outside? Come in! I have made everything ready for you and your camels."

They unloaded and fed the camels and brought water to wash the dusty feet of the servant and his men. But the servant refused to eat anything until he had told his story.

"I am Abraham's servant," he began. "God has blessed my master so that he has become very rich. In their old age, Abraham and his wife, Sarah, had a son, who will inherit everything when Abraham dies. My master made me swear to find a wife for his son from his own family. God sent me a sign and guided me to your daughter."

Then Abraham's servant told Laban and his family all that had happened at the well.

"Now tell me," he said, "will you will act kindly toward my master?"

Laban and his father answered, "The matter was decided by God. Take Rebekah to be the wife of your master's son."

The servant gave Rebekah many gifts—silver and gold, and clothing—and also gave gifts to members of her family. Then the servant and his men had dinner and spent the night.

The next day, the servant said, "Let me return home to my master."

But Rebekah's mother and her brother Laban asked him to stay with them another ten days.

The servant replied, "Do not make me wait. Let me go."

They answered, "Let us ask Rebekah."

When they asked her, "Will you go with this man?" she replied, "I will."

So they sent off Rebekah with Abraham's servant, who then traveled back to Canaan.

Isaac was walking in the field at twilight when he saw camels approaching. When Rebekah saw him, she got off her camel and put on her veil. The servant then told Isaac all that had happened.

Isaac brought Rebekah into the tent of his mother, Sarah, and Rebekah became his wife. Isaac loved her, and he was comforted after his mother's death.

Jacob Steals the Birthright

Genesis 25:19–34; 27:1–28:5

Isaac was 40 years old when he married Rebekah. Over the next 20 years, they had no children. Isaac prayed to God on behalf of his wife. She became pregnant with twins, who struggled with each other inside her.

Rebekah cried out to God, "What is happening to me?"

God told her: "Two nations are inside you, one stronger than the other. The older one will serve the younger."

When Rebekah gave birth, the first twin came out all covered with red hair, so they named him Esau, which means "hairy one." The second twin came out grabbing his brother's heel, so they named him Jacob, which comes from the word meaning "heel." Esau grew up to be a hunter and loved the outdoors. Jacob was a gentle man, who stayed close to the camp. Isaac was fond of hunted game and therefore favored Esau, but Rebekah loved Jacob.

Once when Jacob was cooking lentil stew, Esau came home hungry from the fields.

Esau said to his brother, "Give me some of that red stuff!"

Jacob said, "First sell me your birthright."

Esau replied, "What good to me is my birthright if I die?"

So Esau swore an oath handing over his birthright to his brother Jacob. Then Jacob gave him bread and lentil stew to eat.

So Esau rejected his birthright.

When Isaac was old and blind, he said to his older son, Esau, "Who knows how soon I will die? Go hunt some game and prepare it for me the way I like, so that I may give you my special blessing before I die."

Rebekah was listening to their conversation, and she said to her son Jacob, "I overheard your father tell your brother—'Hunt and prepare some game for me, so that I may bless you before I die.' Now listen to me, and do as I say. Fetch me two fine young goats from the flock, and I will cook them just the way your father likes. Then bring the dish to your father, so that he can bless you before he dies."

Jacob said, "But Esau is a hairy man, and my skin is smooth. If my father touches me, he'll discover my trick. Then he'll curse and not bless me."

His mother replied, "Your curse will be on my head, my son! Just do as I say."

So Rebekah cooked the goats the way Jacob liked. She then dressed Jacob in Esau's best clothes, and covered his neck and hands with the skins from the slaughtered goats. Then she gave Jacob the meat and bread she had prepared, and he brought them to his father.

He said, "Father."

Isaac answered, "Which of my sons are you?"

Jacob said, "I am Esau, your firstborn. Here is the game you asked for. Please sit up and eat, and then bless me."

"How did you succeed so quickly?"

Jacob answered, "God gave me good luck."

Isaac said to Jacob, "Come closer, my son, so that I may touch you, to see whether you are really my son Esau or not." When he touched him, he said, "The voice is the voice of Jacob, but the hands are the hands of Esau."

Isaac asked him again, "Are you really my son Esau?"

Jacob answered, "I am."

After Jacob had served him the meat and given him wine to drink, Isaac said to him, "Come close and kiss me, my son."

Isaac kissed Jacob and smelled his clothes, and then he blessed him.

As soon as Jacob was gone, Esau came back from hunting. He prepared a dish and brought it to his father, and said to him, "Sit up and eat, my father, and give me your blessing."

Isaac said to him, "Who are you?"

He answered, "I am your son, Esau, your firstborn."

Isaac began to tremble. He asked, "Then who was it who brought game to me before? Since I blessed him, he must remain blessed!"

When Esau heard this, he cried wildly and bitterly, and said "Bless me, too, Father!"

Isaac answered, "Your brother tricked me and took away your blessing."

Esau said, "So he has earned his name, Jacob, 'heel,' for he has cheated me out of both my birthright and my blessing. Do you not have a blessing left for me?"

Isaac replied, "I have named him your master and blessed him with grain and wine. What do I have left for you, my son?"

"Surely, you have something," Esau said. "Bless me, too, Father."

Isaac said, "By your sword you will live, and you will serve your brother. But you will rebel and throw off his yoke."

After this, Esau bore a grudge against his brother. He swore to himself, "As soon as my father dies and I have mourned him, I will kill my brother, Jacob."

When Rebekah learned of Esau's plans, she told Jacob to run away to her birthplace where her brother, Laban, still lived.

She said to Jacob, "Stay with Laban until your brother's anger cools, and then I will send for you. Let me not lose you both in one day."

So Jacob left his parents' house and traveled back to his mother's birthplace, to stay with his uncle Laban.

Jacob's Dream

Genesis 28:10–22

Jacob traveled through the desert toward Laban's house. When the sun set that night, he found a place to rest and lay down for the night. He placed a stone under his head and fell asleep.

He dreamed of a ladder that reached from the earth to the sky, with angels going up and down on it. Beside him stood God, who said to him, "I am the God of your father Abraham and the God of Isaac. This ground you now lie upon I give to you and your descendants, who will spread out to the west, east, north, and south. I am with you and will protect you wherever you go, and I will bring you back here to this land."

Jacob woke from his sleep and said, "Surely God is here in this place, and I did not know it! This is none other than God's house, the gateway to heaven."

Jacob took the stone that he had used as a pillow and poured olive oil upon it. He named the place Bethel, which means the "the house of God," and he swore a vow: "God, if You protect me and care for me on this journey, and return me safely to my father's house, You will be my God. This stone will mark Your dwelling place. And I will give back to You one tenth of all that You give me."

Then Jacob continued on his way.

The Trickster Gets Tricked

Genesis 29:1–32:2

Jacob reached the region where Laban lived and came to a well covered by a large stone. Each night when all the flocks gathered by this well, the shepherds of the region would roll the stone from the mouth of this well and water their sheep. When Jacob arrived at the well, three flocks of sheep were lying nearby.

Jacob asked the shepherds, "Do you know Laban, son of Nahor?"

"Yes, we do," they replied, "and here comes his daughter Rachel with her flock."

Jacob said to the shepherds, "Will you roll off the stone covering the mouth of the well?"

"No," they said. "It's still broad daylight, too early to round up all our flocks and water them."

So Jacob rolled off the stone by himself and watered Rachel's flock. He then kissed Rachel and burst into tears, telling her that he was her cousin Rebekah's son. Rachel ran and told her father, who ran to greet his nephew Jacob and bring him home.

Laban said to him, "You are truly my flesh and blood."

Jacob stayed with Laban for a month. Then Laban said to Jacob, "Why should you work without pay just because you're my flesh and flood? Tell me what I should pay you."

Jacob replied, "I will serve you seven years for the hand of your daughter Rachel."

Now Laban had two daughters. Leah, the older daughter, had delicate eyesight. Her younger sister, Rachel, was graceful and fair, and Jacob loved her.

Laban said, "It is better to marry her to you than to a stranger."

So Jacob worked seven years for Rachel, but because he loved her, the years seemed to him like only a few days.

At the end of seven years Jacob said to Laban, "Give me my wife, for I have served my seven years."

So Laban made a feast for all his neighbors.

When it grew dark, Laban brought his older daughter, Leah, to Jacob's tent, and Jacob spent the night with her. When morning came, Jacob was shocked to discover that he was with Leah, not Rachel.

Jacob said to Laban, "Why did you trick me? I served you for Rachel!"

Laban replied, "It's not our custom to marry the younger daughter before the older. When the honeymoon week is over, I'll give you her sister, Rachel, too—if you'll serve me for another seven years."

And so, at the end of the week, Jacob married Rachel as well, and he loved her more than Leah. As wedding gifts, Laban gave Leah his servant Zilpah to be her maid and gave Rachel his servant Bilhah to be her maid.

Then Jacob served Laban for another seven years.

When God saw that Leah was unloved, God gave her children—but Rachel was barren. Leah gave birth to four sons: Reuben, Simeon, Levi, and Judah.

Rachel envied her sister, and said to Jacob, "Give me children, or I'll die!"

Jacob was angry with her and said, "Can I play God?"

So Rachel gave Jacob her maid, Bilhah, and said, "I will have children through her."

And Bilhah became pregnant and gave birth to a son, whom Rachel named Dan. Then Bilhah gave birth to a second son, whom Rachel named Naftali.

Leah now gave Jacob her maid, Zilpah. And Zilpah gave birth to a son, whom Leah named Gad, and then she gave birth to a second son, whom Leah named Asher.

Then Leah became pregnant again and gave birth to her fifth son, whom she named Issachar, and a sixth son, whom she called Zebulun.

Then she gave birth to a daughter, whom she named Dinah.

Then God remembered Rachel. And Rachel gave birth to a son, whom she named Joseph.

Jacob worked for Laban for a total of 20 years, and God blessed Jacob and multiplied his flocks.

Then God said to Jacob, "Return to the land of your fathers, and I will be with you."

So Jacob left with his wives, his children, and his flocks, and journeyed back toward Canaan, to meet his brother, Esau.

Jacob Wrestles with an Angel

Genesis 32:4–13, 23–33; 33:1–4

Jacob sent messengers ahead to his brother, Esau.

The messengers returned and said, "Your brother is coming to meet you, and with him are 400 men."

Jacob was very much afraid. He divided his family, servants, and flocks into two camps so that he would not lose all that he had if his brother attacked. He prayed to God to protect him from his brother and to remember the divine promise to make Jacob's descendants as numerous as the sands of the sea.

The next morning Jacob sent his brother, Esau, many animals from his flocks as gifts, hoping to soften his brother's anger.

That night Jacob crossed the river Jabbok with his wives, his children, and all his possessions. Then he crossed back to the opposite bank, where he remained alone.

Then a man appeared and wrestled with Jacob until sunrise.

When the man saw that he could not overpower Jacob, he pulled Jacob's hip out of its socket, and said, "Let me go, for the sun is rising."

But Jacob said, "I will not let you go until you bless me."

The man asked Jacob, "What is your name?"

He replied, "Jacob."

"Your name will no longer be Jacob," the man said, "but Israel, *Yisra'el,* for you have wrestled—*sareeta*—with God and with human beings, and have won."

"Please tell me your name," said Jacob.

"You must not ask my name!" the man said.

And then he left.

As the sun rose, Jacob went on his way, limping. That is why to this day Jews do not eat an animal's thigh muscle that is attached to the hip socket, because that is where Jacob was wounded when he wrestled that night.

Esau came to meet his brother, Jacob, and embraced him, and both of them wept.

Then Jacob left his brother and continued on his way, together with his wives, his children, his servants, and his flocks.

Joseph the Dreamer

Genesis 37

When Jacob's son Joseph was 17 years old, he helped tend his father's flocks with his brothers. Joseph would tell his father spiteful stories about his brothers.

Now Jacob loved Joseph best of all his sons because he was the child of his old age. Jacob made Joseph a coat of many colors. When Joseph's brothers saw that their father loved Joseph more than any of them, they hated him and would not speak a friendly word to him.

Once Joseph had a dream, which he told to his brothers, and they hated him even more.

He said to them, "There we were tying up sheaves of grain in the field, when suddenly my sheaf stood up, and your sheaves gathered around mine and bowed down to my sheaf."

His brothers replied, "Do you expect to rule over us?"

And they hated him even more.

Then Joseph told them about a second dream: "In this dream, the sun, the moon, and eleven stars were bowing down to me."

When he told this dream to his father and brothers, his father scolded him, saying, "What is this dream you have dreamed? That your mother and I and your brothers will one day bow down to you?"

His brothers resented him, and his father took note of that.

One day, when his brothers had taken their father's flock out to pasture, Jacob sent for Joseph.

Joseph said, "Here I am."

His father said, "Go see how your brothers and the flocks are doing and bring me back a report."

When Joseph's brothers saw him coming in the distance, they plotted to kill him. They said to each other, "Here comes that dreamer! Let's kill him and throw him into one of the dry water pits. Then we can say, 'A wild beast has eaten him up.' So much for his dreams!"

But when Reuben, the oldest brother, heard what they were saying, he tried to save Joseph.

"Let us not take his life," he said, "or spill any blood! Let us throw him into a pit. But let us not raise our own hands against him."

Although the others did not know it, Reuben planned to save Joseph later and bring him back to his father.

When Joseph reached his brothers, they stripped off his coat of many colors, and threw him into an empty water pit. Then they sat down to eat. When they looked up, they saw a caravan of Ishmaelites, carrying spices down to Egypt.

Judah said to his brothers, "What do we gain by killing our brother and hiding his blood? Let's sell him as a slave to these Ishmaelites, rather than raise our own hands against him. For he's our brother, our own flesh and blood."

His brothers agreed.

So they sold Joseph as a slave for 20 pieces of silver, and the Ishmaelites brought Joseph down to Egypt.

When Reuben returned to the pit and saw that Joseph was gone, he tore his clothes. He went to his brothers and said, "The boy's gone! Now what shall I do?"

They took Joseph's coat, slaughtered a young goat, and dipped the coat in its blood. Then they sent the coat of many colors to their father, and said, "We found this. Do you recognize it?"

Jacob recognized it, and said, "My son's coat! A wild beast has eaten him up. It has torn Joseph to pieces."

Jacob tore his clothes and put on coarse mourning cloth, and mourned his son for many days. His children all tried to comfort him, but he refused to be comforted, saying, "I will go down to my grave mourning my son."

Joseph was sold in Egypt to Potiphar, chief steward in Pharaoh's court.

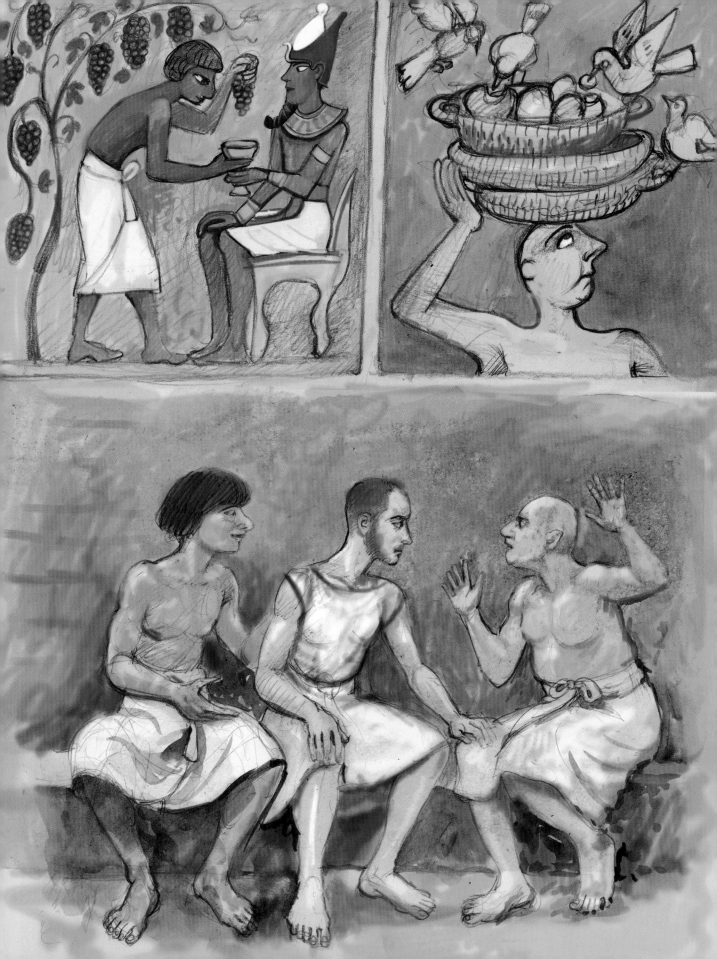

From Slave to Viceroy

Genesis 39:1–41:57

Joseph became a servant in Potiphar's house. God was with Joseph, and he prospered in the house of his Egyptian master. When Potiphar saw that God blessed Joseph in everything he did, Potiphar put Joseph in charge of his entire household and all that he owned, inside and outside. For Joseph's sake, God blessed Potiphar and all that he owned. So Potiphar left Joseph in charge of everything, except the food that he ate.

Now Joseph was graceful and fair. Potiphar's wife had her eye on Joseph, and one day she said to him, "Come to me."

But Joseph refused.

He said to her, "Look, my master trusts me so much that I know better than he does what is in his own house. I have as much authority in his house as he has. He has not denied me anything—except you, his wife. How could I do such a wicked thing and sin before God?"

She pleaded with Joseph every day, but he refused to go off alone with her.

One day, Joseph came into the house to do his work. Knowing that no one else was there, Potiphar's wife grabbed onto Joseph's cloak.

Joseph ran outside, leaving his cloak behind in her hand.

She called to her servants, "See, my husband brought a Hebrew slave here to toy with me! He tried to lay his hands on me but I screamed. So he ran away, leaving his cloak behind in my hand."

She held on to Joseph's cloak until her husband came home. Then she told him the same story. When Potiphar heard what his servant had done, he was furious. He had Joseph thrown into the dungeon where the king's prisoners were kept.

And God was with Joseph there. The warden took a liking to Joseph and put him in charge of all the other prisoners and all that went on there. God made Joseph successful in all that he did.

Some time afterwards, the royal cupbearer and the royal baker offended Pharaoh. He had them thrown into prison, where they were placed under Joseph's charge.

After the two servants had been in custody for some time, each dreamed a dream on the same night. When Joseph came to them the next morning, he saw that they were troubled.

He asked them, "Why are you so unhappy today?"

They answered, "Each of us dreamed a dream, and there is no one to interpret them for us."

Joseph said to them, "God can interpret dreams. Tell them to me."

So the cupbearer told Joseph his dream: "In my dream there was a vine with three branches. Blossoms suddenly appeared on the bare branches, and they then ripened into grapes. Pharaoh's cup was in my hand, and I took the grapes, pressed them into the cup, and handed the cup to Pharaoh."

Joseph said to him, "Here is the meaning of your dream: The three branches are three days. Three days from now, Pharaoh will pardon you and restore you to your place as his cupbearer. Please, when all is well with you again, remember to tell Pharaoh about me so I can be freed from this place. For I was kidnapped from the land of the Hebrews, and I have done nothing to deserve being thrown in this pit."

When the chief baker saw how well the dream had turned out for the cupbearer, he said to Joseph: "In my dream, there were three baskets on my head, and in the top basket were all kinds of baked goods prepared for Pharaoh. Birds were eating these from the basket on my head."

Joseph said to him, "Here is the meaning of your dream: The three baskets are three days. Three days from now, Pharaoh will hang you from a tree, and the birds will eat your flesh."

Three days later was Pharaoh's birthday, and he made a banquet for all his servants. He restored the chief cupbearer to his former place, and he hanged the chief baker—just as Joseph had said.

But the chief cupbearer forgot all about Joseph.

Two years later, Pharaoh dreamed a dream: He was standing by the Nile River, and out of the river came seven cows, handsome and healthy, and they grazed among the reeds. Soon after, out of the Nile came seven other cows, ugly and thin, and these stood on the banks of the Nile next to the first seven cows. And the ugly, thin cows ate up the handsome, healthy cows. Then Pharaoh woke up.

Pharaoh fell asleep and dreamed again: Seven ears of grain, plump and healthy, grew on a single stalk. But seven other ears, shriveled and scorched by the east wind, soon sprouted up. And the seven shriveled ears swallowed up the healthy ears.

Then Pharaoh woke up. It was all a dream!

The next morning, Pharaoh awoke with a troubled spirit. He sent for all the magicians and wise men of Egypt, and he told them his dreams, but none could tell Pharaoh what they meant.

Then the chief cupbearer spoke up: "Some time ago Pharaoh became angry with me and the chief baker and had us thrown into prison. While we were imprisoned there, each of us dreamed a dream on the same night. We told our dreams to a young Hebrew prisoner, a servant of Pharaoh's chief steward, Potiphar, and he interpreted our dreams for us. And what he told us came true: I was restored to my place, and the baker was hanged."

Pharaoh sent for Joseph. He was quickly shaved and dressed in new clothes, and presented to Pharaoh.

Pharaoh said to him, "I have dreamed a dream, and no one can interpret it. I have heard that you can interpret dreams."

Joseph replied, "God, not I, will help you."

So Pharaoh told Joseph his dreams of the seven cows and the seven ears of grain.

Joseph said to him, "This is but a single dream. The seven good cows and the seven good ears stand for seven years. The seven thin cows and the seven empty ears also mean seven years. God has shown Pharaoh what is about to happen: The next seven years will be times of plenty in the land of Egypt. But they will be followed by seven years of famine. Because Pharaoh has had the same dream twice, it means that this is the will of God, and that it will happen soon.

"Therefore, let Pharaoh look for a wise man and put him in charge of the land of Egypt. Let him also appoint officials to collect food during the good years and store it in reserve in the cities. If you do this, Egypt will survive the years of famine."

Joseph's plan pleased Pharaoh and his officials.

Pharaoh said to them, "Could we ever find any one else like this man, who is filled with the spirit of God?"

Then Pharaoh said to Joseph, "Since God has revealed all this to you, there is no one as wise as you! You shall be in charge of my court. My people will be directed by your command. Only my throne will be above you. I put you in charge of the whole land of Egypt."

Then Pharaoh took off his signet ring and placed it on Joseph's finger. He had Joseph clothed in fine linen robes, and he placed a golden chain around his neck. Joseph was then driven around in one of the king's chariots, and all the people cheered for him.

Then Pharaoh said to him, "I am still Pharaoh. But only at your command will anyone lift a hand or foot in Egypt."

Then Pharaoh gave Joseph a new name, Zaphenath-paneah, meaning, "creator of life." He also gave him a wife, Asenat, daughter of an Egyptian priest. Joseph was 30 years old when he became viceroy of Egypt.

During the seven years of plenty, Joseph gathered all the grain that the land produced and had it stored in whichever city was closest to the growing fields. So abundant was the grain that it outnumbered the sands of the sea, so Joseph gave up measuring it.

Then Asenat gave birth to two sons. Joseph named his firstborn Manasseh, and his second son, Ephraim.

Then the seven years of abundance came to an end, and the seven years of famine began. There was famine in every land, but in the land of Egypt there was bread. And when the whole land of Egypt felt the famine and cried out to Pharaoh for bread, Pharaoh said to them, "Go to Joseph, and he will tell you what to do."

When the famine became very bad in Egypt, Joseph opened up the storehouses and rationed out grain to the Egyptians. But the famine spread over the whole world, and from all over they came to Joseph in Egypt for rations.

Joseph Tests His Brothers

Genesis 42–50

And famine struck in the land of Canaan.

When Jacob saw that there was food in Egypt, he said to his sons, "Go down to Egypt and get rations for us, so that we may live and not die."

So ten of Joseph's brothers went down to Egypt. But Jacob did not send Benjamin, his youngest son and Joseph's brother, with them, for he feared that the boy might come to harm.

Joseph's brothers came before Joseph, viceroy of Egypt, and bowed before him. When Joseph saw his brothers, he recognized them, but they did not recognize him. He acted like a stranger toward them and spoke to them harshly.

He said to them, "Where do you come from?"

They answered, "From the land of Canaan. We have come for food."

Then Joseph remembered the dreams he had had about them.

He said to them, "You are spies! You have come to spy on us when we are weak."

They said, "No, my lord, we have come only for food. We are honest men, not spies."

He said to them, "No, you have come to spy!"

They said, "We are 12 brothers, all sons of one man in the land of Canaan. Our youngest brother is still with our father—and one brother is no more."

Joseph said to them, "No, you are spies. And this is how I will test you: either you bring your youngest brother to me or you will not leave here. One of you shall return home and bring your brother back, and the rest of you will remain here in prison. In this way I will test whether you are telling the truth—or are spies."

Then he had them locked up in the guardhouse.

After three days, Joseph said to them, "Do this and you will live, for I am a God-fearing man. If you really are honest men, let one of your brothers stay here in custody while the rest of you bring home rations to your starving families. But you must bring your youngest brother back to me. Then I will believe your story, and you will not die."

The brothers said to each other, "We're now paying for what we did to our brother Joseph. When we saw his distress, we paid no attention to his pleas. That's why we are now in distress ourselves."

Then Reuben said to them, "Didn't I say to you, 'Don't harm the boy?' But you wouldn't listen to me, and now we must pay for his blood."

When he heard their words, Joseph turned his back to them to hide his tears. Then he singled out Simeon and had him bound and held in prison.

Joseph then ordered his servants to place rations in their sacks, to secretly return their money to them, and to provide them with additional food for their journey. So it was done.

The brothers then loaded up their donkeys and went on their way.

That night when they reached a resting place, one of them opened up his sack to feed his donkey and discovered that his money had been returned to his sack.

He said to his brothers, "My money has been returned to me—here it is in my sack!"

They began to tremble, saying to each other, "What has God done to us!"

When they came to their father, Jacob, in the land of Canaan, they told him all that had happened to them: "The lord of that land spoke harshly to us and accused us of being spies. He said to us, 'I will know you are honest men only if you leave one of your brothers here with me, take food home for your starving families, and then return here with your youngest brother. Then I will know that you are not spies, and I will release your brother to you, and you will be free to go.'"

When they now emptied their sacks, they discovered that all of their moneybags had been returned to them. When they saw this, they and their father were distressed.

Jacob said, "You are always taking from me! Joseph is gone and so is Simeon, and now you want to take Benjamin away, too!"

Then Reuben said to his father, "You can kill my own two sons if I do not bring Benjamin back to you. Give him to me, and I will return him to you."

But Jacob said, "No, my youngest son will not go down with you. His brother Joseph is dead, and he is all I have left. If he meets with disaster on the way, you will send me to my grave."

But the famine was very bad in Canaan. When Jacob's family had eaten up all the food they had brought from Egypt, their father Jacob said to them, "Go back and get more food for us."

But Judah said, "The man warned us, 'Do not show your faces here again unless you bring your brother with you.' Now if you will let Benjamin go with us, we will go down and get food for you. But if not, we will not go down, for the man said that he would not see us without Benjamin."

Jacob said, "Why did you do this to me, telling the man that you had one more brother?"

They said, "The man kept asking us about ourselves and our family, wanting to know: 'Is your father still alive? Do you have another brother?'

73

We answered the questions he asked us. How were we to know that he would say to us, 'Bring your brother here'?"

Then Judah said to his father, "Send the boy with me. Let us be on our way before we die, we and our little ones. I myself will be responsible for the boy. If I do not bring him back to you, I'll stand guilty before you forever."

Then Jacob said to them, "If it must be so, then take as gifts some of the finest produce of our land—perfume and honey, spices and incense, pistachios and almonds. Also take with you double the money, so that you can return the money you found in your sacks. Perhaps it was a mistake. Take your youngest brother as well, and go back at once to the man. May God move him to act kindly toward you so that he releases your other brother as well as Benjamin."

So they took with them the gifts, the double amount of money, and Benjamin, and they went down to Egypt and stood before Pharaoh. When Joseph saw Benjamin with them, he said to his house steward, "Bring these men into my house. Then prepare an animal for us to eat, for these men will dine with me at noon."

The brothers were frightened to be brought to Joseph's house, for they thought, "It's because of the money we found in our sacks. He's brought us here to seize us as his slaves, together with our animals."

So they said to Joseph's house steward, "My lord, we came down once before to get food rations. But on our way home, when we looked in our sacks, we found all our money returned to us, and we do not know who put it there. Now we have come down again, ready to repay what was returned to us and to pay additional money for more food."

He said to them, "Do not be afraid. All is well. Your God and the God of your fathers must have put treasure in your sacks. I have already received your money."

Then he brought Simeon out to them.

They were then brought into Joseph's house, where they were given water to wash their feet, and feed for their animals. Then they laid out their gifts and waited for Joseph.

When Joseph came home, they presented their gifts to him and bowed down before him.

He said to them, "How is your old father that you spoke about? Is he still alive?"

They answered, "Yes, he is well." And they bowed again.

Then he looked around and saw his brother Benjamin, his mother's only other son, and he said, "Is this your youngest brother whom you told me about?" And he said to Benjamin, "May God be good to you, my son."

Then Joseph hurried out, for he was filled with such tender feeling toward his brother that he was about to cry. He went into another room and cried there. Then he washed his face and returned, in control of himself again. He ordered his servants to serve the meal.

To the brothers' astonishment, Joseph arranged for them to be seated in their correct birth order, from the oldest brother to the youngest. They all received portions from Joseph's table—but Benjamin's portion was larger than the others'. They ate and drank their fill.

Then Joseph instructed his house steward: "Fill their sacks with food, as much as they can carry, and put their money back in their sacks. In the sack of the youngest one put my silver goblet, together with his money."

The steward did as Joseph ordered.

Early the next morning, the brothers left with their pack animals, but they had not gone far before Joseph said to his steward, "Go after these men! When you catch up with them, say to them, 'Why have you repaid good with evil? The goblet you have stolen is the one my master uses for divining the future. Stealing it was a wicked thing to do!"

When the steward caught up with them, he repeated his master's words.

The brothers answered him, "Why does my lord say such things? We

would never act in this way! See, we have brought back the money we found in our bags the last time. Why would we steal silver or gold from your master's house? Go ahead and search our sacks. If you find the stolen goblet in one of them, sentence that man to death and make the rest of us your slaves."

The steward said to them, "Only the one who has taken the goblet will become my master's slave. The rest of you will go free."

Then each brother opened his sack. The steward searched them all, and found the goblet in Benjamin's sack. When the brothers saw this, they tore their clothes in grief. Then they rode their donkeys back to the city.

When the brothers came back into Joseph's house, they threw themselves on the ground before him.

Joseph said to them, "What have you done? Do you not realize that a man like me can see into the future?"

Judah answered, "What can we say to you, my lord? God has exposed our crime. We are now your slaves. Each one of us is as guilty as the one in whose sack the goblet was found."

Joseph said, "No, only the one who took the goblet will be my slave. The rest of you, go home in peace to your father."

Then Judah went up to Joseph and said, "Please, my lord, you who are the equal of Pharaoh, do not be impatient with me when I speak with you now. When my lord asked us, 'Do you have a father or another brother?' we told you, 'We have an old father and a little brother, the child of his old age, whose other full brother has died. Our father dotes on him.' And you said to us, 'Bring him down to me so I can see him.' We said to you, 'The boy cannot leave his father, for if he does, his father will die.' But you said to us, 'If he does not come down, you will not see my face again.' And when we told this to my father, he said to us, 'My wife Rachel gave me only two sons. One was torn apart by wild beasts, and I have not seen him since. If you take the other one from me as well, and something happens to him, you'll send my white head in sorrow down to the grave.'

"Now if we return home without the boy, my father—whose life is tied up with his—will surely die. I have sworn to my father that I myself will be responsible for the boy. If I do not bring him back, I will remain guilty before my father forever. Please take me as your slave instead of the boy and let the boy go back with his brothers. For how can I go back to my father unless the boy is with me? I could not bear to see my father's sorrow."

Joseph could no longer control himself. He ordered all his servants to leave the room. His crying was so loud that all the Egyptians could hear.

Joseph said to his brothers, "I am Joseph. Is my father still alive?"

But his brothers could not answer him, for they were struck dumb.

Then Joseph said to his brothers, "Come closer."

When they came closer, he said to them, "I am your brother Joseph, whom you sold into Egypt. Do not be upset that you sold me, for it was to save lives and redeem you that God sent me here ahead of you. It was not you who sent me here but God, who has made me second to Pharaoh, the lord of all his house, and ruler over the whole land of Egypt.

"Now hurry home to my father and tell him: 'So says your son Joseph: "God has made me lord over Egypt. Come down to me without delay. You will live in the land of Goshen and be near me—you, your children and your grandchildren, and your sheep and cattle and all that you have. I will take care of you during the remaining five years of famine, so that you and all who are with you will not go hungry." ' Go to my father and tell him everything you've seen here, and bring him here as soon as possible."

Then he embraced his brother Benjamin, and they cried together. He kissed all of his brothers and cried with them. Only then were they finally able to speak.

The news reached Pharaoh's palace: Joseph's brothers have come. The news pleased Pharaoh and his court.

Pharaoh said to Joseph, "Tell your brothers: 'Load up your animals and go to the land of Canaan at once. Bring your father and your families down to Egypt, and I will give you the best of the land of Egypt. Bring wagons with you for your children and wives, but do not bother with your possessions, for the best of the land will be yours.'"

So Joseph gave them wagons as well as food and clothing for the journey. To Benjamin he gave 300 pieces of silver and several changes of clothing. To his father he sent 20 donkeys loaded with the best things of Egypt.

And as he sent off his brothers, he told them, "Do not fight with each other on the way."

They came to their father Jacob in the land of Canaan. They said to him, "Joseph is still alive, and he rules over the whole land of Egypt."

Then Jacob's heart went numb, for he did not believe them. But when they told him all that Joseph had said to them, and when he saw the wagons Joseph had sent, his spirit recovered.

Jacob said, "Enough! My son Joseph is still alive. I must go and see him before I die."

So Jacob and all who were with him set out for Egypt. Those who left Canaan with Jacob and those who were already in Egypt numbered 70.

Along the way God came to Jacob in a night vision, and said, "I am the God of your fathers. Do not be afraid to go down to Egypt, for I will make you a great nation there. I Myself will go down with you to Egypt and I Myself will bring you back, and Joseph's hand will close your eyes."

When they arrived in Egypt, Joseph rode out in his chariot to meet his father, and they embraced each other and cried for a long time.

Jacob said to Joseph, "Now I can die, for I have seen for myself that you are still alive."

Jacob lived in Egypt for 17 more years. When he died, Joseph closed his eyes.

And as Joseph had promised his father, he brought Jacob's body back to Canaan, to bury him in the cave of Machpelah next to his ancestors, Abraham and Sarah, Isaac and Rebekah, and Leah. But Jacob's wife Rachel was not buried there, for she had died on the way to Canaan, giving birth to Benjamin, and had been buried beside the road.

Joseph lived to see his great-great-grandchildren. When he reached the age of 110 and was about to die, he said to his brothers: "In future years, God will take note of you and bring you out of Egypt to the land promised to Abraham, Isaac, and Jacob. And when you leave, carry my bones with you."

Then Joseph died and was embalmed and was placed in a coffin in Egypt.

Pharaoh and the Hebrew Midwives

Exodus 1:7–22

Many years passed. The Israelites multiplied in Egypt and filled the land.

Then a new Pharaoh came to the throne who did not know about Joseph.

Pharaoh said to his people, "Look, the Israelites are too many for us. Let us act so that they cannot increase in number. Otherwise, when we go to war, they will join our enemies and fight against us."

So they forced the Israelites to work as slaves, building treasury cities for Pharaoh. But the more that the Israelites were beaten down, the more they multiplied until the Egyptians grew afraid of them.

Then Pharaoh spoke to the Hebrew midwives, Shifrah and Puah, and said to them, "From now on, when you help an Israelite woman to give birth, if it is a boy, you must kill him. But if it is a girl, let her live."

But the midwives were faithful to God and did not obey Pharaoh's instructions. They let the boys live.

So Pharaoh sent for the midwives and said to them, "Why have you done this, letting the boys live?"

The midwives answered, "The Hebrew women are not like the Egyptian women. They are remarkably strong. Before we can even come to them, they have already given birth!"

And God took care of the midwives so that their families prospered. And the Israelites continued to multiply.

Then Pharaoh commanded his own people, "Every Hebrew boy that is born you shall throw into the Nile, but let every girl live."

The Birth of Moses

Exodus 2:1–10

Amram, an Israelite from the House of Levi, married Jochebed, also from the House of Levi. And Jochebed gave birth to a son. When she saw how beautiful he was, she hid the baby for three months. When she could no longer hide him, she took a small ark made of reeds, caulked it with pitch, and placed the child in it. Then she set it afloat among the reeds along the banks of the Nile. Miriam, the baby's sister, watched from a distance, to see what would happen to the child.

Pharaoh's daughter came down to bathe in the Nile. She saw the ark among the reeds and sent her slave girl to bring it to her. When she opened it, she found a baby boy, crying. She took pity on him and said, "This must be one of the Hebrew babies."

Then Miriam said to Pharaoh's daughter, "Should I go and fetch you a Hebrew woman to nurse the child?"

"Yes, go," Pharaoh's daughter answered.

Miriam brought to her Jochebed, the baby's mother.

Pharaoh's daughter said to her, "Take this child, nurse him, and I will pay you."

So Jochebed took her own child and nursed him. And when he was old enough, she brought him to Pharaoh's daughter, who adopted him as her own son.

Pharaoh's daughter named him Moses, *Moshe*, because, she said, "I drew him—*mee-shee-tee-hu*—out of the water."

Moses Flees to Midian

Exodus 2:11–22

Some time later, when Moses was grown up, he went out among his people and saw how hard they worked. He saw an Egyptian beating a Hebrew slave. He looked around, and seeing no one close by, he struck the Egyptian dead and buried his body in the sand.

The next day when Moses went out among the Hebrew slaves, he came upon two of them fighting.

Moses said to the one who was in the wrong, "Why are you beating your fellow Hebrew?"

The man answered, "Who made you lord and master over us? Do you plan to kill me like you killed the Egyptian?"

Then Moses was afraid. He thought, "Surely, everyone must know!"

When Pharaoh learned what Moses had done, he tried to have Moses killed. So Moses ran away to the land of Midian. He came to a well and rested there.

Now Jethro, the priest of Midian, had seven daughters. They came to the well and filled the troughs to water their father's flock. But other shepherds came and drove them away. Moses came to their defense, and he watered their flock.

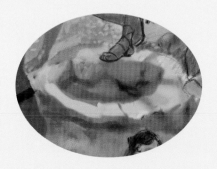

When the seven sisters returned home, their father asked them, "Why are you home so early?"

They answered, "An Egyptian saved us from the other shepherds, and even watered our flock."

"Where is this man?" he asked his daughters. "Why did you leave him there? Bring him home so he can share bread with us."

Moses agreed to stay with Jethro and his family. Jethro gave Moses his daughter Zipporah as his wife. She gave birth to a son, whom Moses named Gershom, saying, "I have been a stranger— *ger*—in a foreign land."

The Burning Bush

Exodus 2:23–4:29

Time passed, and the old Pharaoh died. The Israelite slaves cried out to God because their suffering was very great. God heard their moaning and remembered the covenant with Abraham, Isaac, and Jacob. And God took note of the people.

One day Moses led his father-in-law's flock into the wilderness and came to Horeb, the Mountain of God. There an angel of God appeared to him in a blazing fire in the middle of a bush. He saw that the bush was burning, but it was not burned up by the flames.

Moses said, "I must go look at this strange sight! Why isn't the bush burning up?"

Then God called to Moses out of the bush: "Moses! Moses!"

Moses answered, "Here I am."

God said, "Do not come any closer! Take off your sandals, for you are standing on holy ground. I am the God of your fathers, the God of Abraham, the God of Isaac, and the God of Jacob."

Moses hid his face, for he was afraid to look at God.

God said, "I have seen the suffering of My people in Egypt and have heard their cries. I have come to rescue them from the Egyptians and to bring them to a good land, flowing with milk and honey, the land of Canaan. I have seen how the Egyptians make the Israelites suffer. I will send you now to Pharaoh, and you will free My people from Egypt."

Moses said to God, "Who am I to go before Pharaoh and free the Israelites from Egypt?"

God answered, "I will be with you. And when you have freed the people from Egypt, you will worship Me at this mountain."

Moses said to God, "When I tell the Israelites, 'The God of your fathers has sent me,' they will ask me, 'What is this God's name?' What shall I tell them?"

God said to Moses, "Tell them, 'Ehyeh-Asher-Ehyeh—I-Am-Who-I-Am-Was-Will-Be—has sent me, the God of your ancestors, Abraham, Isaac, and Jacob.' Gather together the elders of Israel and tell them that I have seen their suffering and will lead them out of Egypt to a land flowing with milk and honey. They will listen to you.

"Go with the elders of Israel to Pharaoh and say to him, 'The God of the Hebrews has appeared to us. Therefore, let us make a three-day journey into the wilderness to sacrifice to our God.' But I know that the king of Egypt will refuse to let you go and will release you only when he faces a power greater than his own. So I will stretch out My hand and strike down Egypt with many wonders and miracles. Then he will let you go. But you will not go away empty-handed. Your neighbors will give you silver, gold, and clothing, and thus you will strip Egypt."

"What if they will not listen to me?" said Moses. "What if they say, 'God did not appear to you!'"

God replied, "What is in your hand?"

Moses answered, "A shepherd's staff."

God said, "Throw it to the ground."

So Moses threw it to the ground, and it became a snake.

Then God said to Moses, "Grab the snake by its tail."

Moses did so, and the snake turned back into a staff.

God said, "Now they will believe that the God of Abraham, Isaac, and Jacob has appeared to you."

Then God said, "Put your hand inside your cloak."

Moses did so. When he pulled out his hand, it was crusted with snow-white scales.

Then God said, "Put your hand back inside your cloak."

Moses did so, and when he pulled out his hand a second time, it was again like the rest of his body.

"If they do not believe these signs," said God, "take some water from the Nile, pour it upon dry ground, and the water will turn to blood."

But Moses said, "Please, God, I have never been a man of words. I am slow of speech and tongue-tied."

God said to him, "Who gives man speech? Who makes him dumb or deaf, sighted or blind? Is it not I, God? Now go, and I will be with you as you speak and will tell you what to say."

But Moses said, "Please, God, choose someone else."

God became angry with Moses and said, "Your brother, Aaron, is on his way now to meet you, and he will be happy to see you. I know that he speaks well. I will be with both of you as you speak and will tell you both what to do. You will put words in his mouth, and he will speak to the people on your behalf. He will serve as your mouth, and you will play the role of God to him. Now go back to Egypt, because the men who wished to kill you are now dead. Take this staff with you, to perform My wonders before Pharaoh."

Then Moses went to his father-in-law, Jethro, and said, "Let me go back to my family in Egypt and see how they are doing."

Jethro said, "Go in peace."

Then Moses placed his wife and two sons upon a donkey and headed toward the land of Egypt.

The Ten Plagues

Exodus 4:29–6:1; 7:1–12:42

Moses and Aaron came to speak to the Israelites in Egypt. They told the people all that God had said to Moses. They performed wonders before the people, and the people were convinced.

Then Moses and Aaron came before Pharaoh and said to him, "The God of the Hebrews has appeared to us. Please let us go a distance of three days into the wilderness to worship our God."

But Pharaoh answered them, "You are distracting the people from their work!"

Pharaoh then ordered the taskmasters, "You will no longer provide the slaves with straw to make their bricks. From now on they will have to gather straw for themselves. But do not reduce their daily quota. They are lazy. That is why they want to stop working and go sacrifice to their God. Let them work harder so they will not have time to listen to such false promises."

So the people had to work even harder. And when they did not make their quota of bricks, the taskmasters beat them. Then the Israelite foremen came to Moses and Aaron and said to them, "May God punish you! You have put a sword in the hands of the Egyptians to kill us."

Moses turned to God and said, "Why have you brought harm to Your people? And why did you send me? Ever since I came to Pharaoh to speak in Your name, he has dealt even worse with them. And still You have not freed Your people."

God said to Moses, "You will soon see what I will do to Pharaoh. He will let the people go because of a power greater than his. In fact, he will drive them from his land. Go to Pharaoh and act as God before him, and your brother, Aaron, will serve as your prophet. Tell Pharaoh to let the Israelites leave his land. But I will harden Pharaoh's heart so that he will refuse, and then I will show Egypt that I am God. I will stretch out My hand and bring the Israelites out of their midst."

So Moses and Aaron came before Pharaoh. Moses was 80 years old and Aaron eighty-three when they appeared before Pharaoh. Aaron threw down his staff before Pharaoh and his court, and the staff became a snake. But the Egyptian magicians did the same with their staffs, so that they too became snakes. Then Aaron's staff swallowed up their staffs. But Pharaoh's heart hardened, so that he paid no attention to Moses and Aaron.

Then God said to Moses, "Go to Pharaoh tomorrow morning when he goes down to the Nile and say to him, 'The God of the Hebrews has sent me to say to you, "Let My people go so that they can worship me in the wilderness." But because you will not listen, God will now turn the water of the Nile into blood and all the fish will die and you will no longer be able to drink the water. By this you will know that I am God.' "

Moses and Aaron did just as God commanded: In the presence of Pharaoh and his court, Aaron lifted up his staff and held it over the waters of Egypt. Then he struck the water of the Nile with his staff, and all the waters of Egypt—in the rivers, canals, and ponds, even in jugs of wood and stone—turned to blood. But Pharaoh's magicians did the same with their spells, so Pharaoh returned to his palace, unimpressed. And all the fish in the Nile died, and the river stank. The Egyptians had to dig around the banks of the Nile for water to drink because they could not drink directly from the river.

Seven days later, God said to Moses, "Go to Pharaoh and say to him, 'Let my people go so that they can worship Me. If you refuse, I will bring a plague of frogs out of the Nile, and they will swarm over your palace and fill your bedrooms and beds, your ovens and your kneading bowls.'"

So Aaron held out his staff over the waters of Egypt, and frogs came up and covered the land. But Pharaoh's magicians did the same with their spells, and brought frogs upon the land.

Then Pharaoh summoned Moses and Aaron and said, "Ask God to

remove these frogs, and I will let the people go offer sacrifices to God."

So Moses cried out to God, and the frogs died in the houses, courtyards, and fields. The Egyptians piled them up in heaps until the land stank. But when Pharaoh saw that the plague was over, he hardened his heart and would not listen to Moses and Aaron.

Then God said to Moses, "Tell Aaron to strike the dust of the earth, so that it turns into lice." So Aaron struck the dust with his staff, and lice covered the Egyptians and their animals.

But when Pharaoh's magicians tried to do the same with their spells, they could not. They said to Pharaoh, "Surely this is the finger of God!" But Pharaoh hardened his heart and would not listen to them.

Then God said to Moses, "Early tomorrow morning as Pharaoh comes down to the water, say to him, 'Thus says God, "Let My people go so that they can worship Me. But if you refuse, I will bring upon Egypt a plague of swarming pests, so that the very ground the people walk on will be covered. But I will spare the land of Goshen, where My people live." ' "

God did so. The next day swarms of rats, mice, cockroaches, and other pests invaded Pharaoh's palace, the houses of his court officials and of his people. And the land of Egypt was ruined.

Then Pharaoh called for Moses and Aaron and said to them, "You may sacrifice to your God within Egypt's borders."

But they replied, "We cannot do so, for the animals that we sacrifice to our God are offensive to the Egyptians, and they will surely stone us! No, we

must go a distance of three days into the wilderness to sacrifice to God as we've been commanded."

Pharaoh said, "Then I will let you go—but not too far. And I beg you to plead on my behalf."

So Moses pleaded with God to remove the swarming pests, and God removed them the next day. Not one remained. But Pharaoh hardened his heart and still refused to let the people go.

Then God said to Moses, "Go tell Pharaoh: 'Thus says the God of the Hebrews, "Let my people go to worship Me. If you refuse to let them go, I will strike down your livestock—your horses, donkeys, camels, cows, and sheep in the fields—with a terrible illness. But I will spare the livestock of the Hebrews."'"

The next day, God did so: All the livestock of the Egyptians died, but not one of the animals belonging to the Hebrews perished.

But Pharaoh's heart remained unmoved, and he would not let the people go.

Then God said to Moses and Aaron, "Take handfuls of soot from the kiln and throw soot up toward the sky. It will turn into a fine dust that will cover the land and cause boils to break out on the Egyptians and their beasts."

Moses and Aaron did so. Boils broke out on all the Egyptians and their animals. But God hardened Pharaoh's heart, and he would not change his mind.

Then God said to Moses, "Appear before Pharaoh early tomorrow morning and say to him, 'Thus says the God of the Hebrews, "Let My people go to worship Me. Though I could have destroyed every one of you with disease, I have kept you alive so you can see My power. Yet you still refuse to let My people go! This time tomorrow I will rain down sheets of hail, such as has never been seen since the dawn of Egypt. Bring your animals indoors and find shelter for yourselves, for everything outside will be destroyed by the hail."'"

Those among Pharaoh's officials who feared God brought their servants and livestock indoors; those who did not left them in the open. Then Moses held out his staff toward the sky, and God sent thunder. Then hail rained down in a stream of fire. Throughout the land of Egypt the hail struck down all that was in the open—the Egyptians and their animals, and all the grasses and trees of the field. Only in the land of Goshen, where the Israelites lived, no hail fall.

Then Pharaoh sent for Moses and Aaron and said to them, "God is right, and I and my people are in the wrong. Plead with God to end this thunder and hail, and I will let you go."

Moses said, "I will do as you ask, and God will take away the thunder and hail. But I know that you and your court do not yet fear God."

So Moses went outside the city and spread out his hands, and the thunder and hail ended. But when Pharaoh saw this, he hardened his heart and would not let the Israelites go.

Then God said to Moses, "Go to Pharaoh. I have hardened his heart so that I can display My wonders before the Egyptians. One day you will tell your children and your children's children how I disgraced the Egyptians by displaying My wonders before them, so that you can know that I am God."

So Moses and Aaron appeared before Pharaoh and said to him, "Thus says the God of the Hebrews, 'How long will you refuse to bow before Me? Let my people go to worship Me. But if you refuse to let them go, I will bring locusts that will eat up any grain left over from the hail, and they will eat up all the trees in the field.' " Now the flax and barley crops were already ruined, but the wheat was not damaged, because it ripens late.

After Moses left, Pharaoh's officials said to him, "How long will you let this man hold us hostage? At least let the men go worship their God! Don't you see that Egypt is lost?"

So Pharaoh summoned Moses and Aaron again and said to them, "Go worship your God. But who among you needs to go?"

"We will all go," Moses replied, "young and old, our sons and our daughters, our flocks and our herds. For we must all celebrate God's festival."

But Pharaoh said to him, "No, only the men will go to worship God, for that is what you have been demanding. Why should your children go— unless you mean to make trouble?"

And he drove them from his sight.

Then Moses held out his arm over the land, and God sent an east wind which blew over the land all that day and all that night. When morning came, locusts invaded, darkening the face of Egypt. Never before had there been so many locusts in the land, nor will there ever be so many again. They hid all the land from view, and the ground was blackened. They ate up all the grasses of the field and all the fruit of the trees that had been spared by the hail, so that nothing green was left in all of Egypt.

Pharaoh quickly sent for Moses and Aaron and said to them, "I have sinned before God and before you. Forgive me this once and plead with your God to remove this death from me."

So Moses pleaded with God, and God brought a strong west wind that drove the locusts into the sea. Not a single locust remained in all the land of Egypt. But God again hardened Pharaoh's heart, and he would not let the Israelites go.

Then God said to Moses, "Stretch out your arm toward the sky so that darkness descends upon Egypt, a darkness so thick that it can be touched."

So Moses held out his arm, and a thick darkness descended upon the land of Egypt for three days. During that time people could not see each another, and no one got up from where he sat. Only the Israelites had light in their dwellings.

Pharaoh then called Moses and said, "Go worship your God! Even your children can go with you. But your flocks and herds shall be left behind."

Moses replied, "You yourself must supply us with animals for our sacrifices. And we will also bring our own livestock with us—not one beast shall remain behind. For we will not know until we arrive what God will demand as a sacrifice."

Then God hardened Pharaoh's heart, and he would not let them go.

Pharaoh said to Moses, "Leave me! See to it that you do not see my face again, for on that day, you will die."

Moses answered, "You are right. I will not see your face again."

Then God said to Moses, "I will bring one last plague upon Pharaoh and Egypt. After that, he will let you go. In fact, he will drive you away. When he does, tell the people to ask their neighbors for objects of silver and gold."

Then God softened the hearts of the Egyptians toward the Israelites, especially toward Moses. Both the members of Pharaoh's court and the people admired Moses throughout the land of Egypt.

Then Moses said to Pharaoh, "Thus says God, 'Near midnight I will go out among the Egyptians, and every firstborn among them will die, from the firstborn of Pharaoh to the firstborn of the slave girl, and all the firstborn of the cattle. And a loud cry will go up from Egypt, such as has never been

heard nor ever will be heard again. But as for the Israelites, not even a dog will snarl at them.' Then everyone in Pharaoh's court will bow before me and will order us to leave. And then we will go."

But God hardened Pharaoh's heart so that he would not let the people go.

Then God said to Moses and Aaron, "Tell the Israelites to take one lamb for each family. At twilight on the 14th day of the month of Nisan, they shall slaughter the lamb and place some of its blood on the doorposts of their houses. Then they will eat the roasted meat, together with unleavened bread and bitter herbs. They must eat quickly, with sandals on their feet and a staff in their hands. For on that night I will strike dead every firstborn of Egypt. But I will pass over the houses of the Israelites that are marked with blood."

Moses told the elders of Israel to pick out lambs for their families and to slaughter them for the Passover sacrifice. He instructed them to take bundles of red hyssop plants and use them to brush the lamb's blood on their doorposts, so that the Destroying Angel would pass over the houses of the Israelites when striking down the Egyptians.

Moses said, "You will observe this Festival of Unleavened Bread for all time, you and your descendants. When your children ask you, 'What do you mean by all this?' you will say to them, 'It is the Festival of Passover, because God passed over the houses of the Israelites in Egypt, but struck down the Egyptians, and so our lives were saved.'"

And the Israelites did all that God had commanded.

And it came to pass in the middle of the night that God struck dead all the firstborn of Egypt, from the firstborn of Pharaoh who sat on the throne to the firstborn of the prisoner in the dungeon as well as all the firstborn of the herds. Pharaoh rose up in the night together with his court and all his people, and a loud cry went forth out of Egypt, for there was not a single house without someone dead.

That night Pharaoh summoned Moses and Aaron and said, "Get out of my land, you and the Israelites with you! Go, worship your God as you have demanded. Take your flocks and your herds—and leave. And may you bless me, too."

All the Egyptians urged the Israelites to leave quickly, for they said, "We will soon all be dead!"

The Israelites took their dough before it had time to rise, and they placed their kneading bowls upon their shoulders. And as Moses had instructed them, they asked their Egyptian neighbors for objects of silver and gold, as well as clothing. God caused the Egyptians to act kindly toward them, so that they gave the Israelites what they asked for. And so the Israelites stripped the Egyptians.

So after 430 years of living in Egypt, all the Israelites together with a mixed host of other people, adults as well as children, and much livestock went out of Egypt. They baked unleavened bread, because they were driven out of Egypt in a great hurry and did not have time to prepare food for the journey.

That night, when God redeemed the Children of Israel from Egypt, was a time of watchfulness. And so it will be throughout the ages—a night of watchfulness for all the Children of Israel.

The Splitting of the Sea of Reeds

Exodus 13:17–15:21

When Pharaoh let the Israelites go, God did not lead them by the shorter route, by the land of the Philistines, but instead took them the long way around, by the wilderness route along the Sea of Reeds.

For God said, "When the people face war, they may have a change of heart and want to return to Egypt."

When the Israelites left Egypt, Moses took with him the bones of Joseph, who had made the Children of Israel swear an oath, saying, "When God takes note of you and takes you out of Egypt, carry my bones away with you."

By day God led them with a pillar of cloud, and by night, with a pillar of fire, so that they could travel day and night. These pillars never left them. And so they came to the edge of the wilderness and camped facing the sea.

God said to Moses, "Pharaoh will now say, 'See, they have lost their way. They are boxed in by the wilderness.' And I will harden Pharaoh's heart, and he will come after you. Then I will achieve glory through Pharaoh and his army, and Egypt will at last know that I am the Lord."

When Pharaoh learned that the Israelites were gone, he said, "What have we done, freeing this people?"

He assembled 600 chariots and officers, horsemen, and warriors, and they chased after the Israelites. They reached the Israelites while they were camped by the sea.

When the Israelites saw the Egyptians approaching, they were frightened and they cried out to God.

They said to Moses, "Were there no graves in Egypt? Have you brought us into the wilderness only to die? What have you done to us, taking us out of Egypt? Did we not tell you while we were still in Egypt: 'Leave us alone to serve the Egyptians, for it is better for us to serve them than to die in the wilderness!'"

But Moses said to them, "Do not be afraid! Wait and see how God will save you today. For the Egyptians you see today you will never see again. God will fight for you—only be still!"

Then God said to Moses, "Why do you cry out to Me? Tell the Israelites to go forward. Hold your staff out over the sea and split it, so that the people can march into the sea on dry land. And I will harden the hearts of the Egyptians so that they will pursue the Israelites. Then the Egyptians will know that I am the Lord, for I will achieve glory through Pharaoh, his chariots and his horsemen."

Then the angel of God who had been leading the Israelite army moved to its rear, and the pillar of cloud also moved behind the people, so that it came between the army of Egypt and the army of Israel. And the cloud of darkness held them all spellbound that night, so that neither army came near the other all night.

Then Moses stretched his arm out over the sea, and God drove back the waters with a strong east wind all night, so that the sea turned into dry land, and the waters were split apart. The Israelites walked into the sea on dry land, and the waters formed a wall to their right and to their left.

Then the Egyptians pursued them into the sea, all of Pharaoh's horses, chariots, and horsemen. At sunrise, God looked down upon the Egyptian army from the pillar of fire and cloud and threw the Egyptian army into a panic, locking their chariot wheels so that they had trouble advancing in the mud.

The Egyptians cried, "Let us flee from the Israelites, for God is fighting for them against Egypt."

Then God said to Moses, "Stretch your arm out over the sea, so that the waters crash down upon the Egyptians, their chariots, and their horsemen."

At sunrise, Moses stretched his arm out over the sea, and the sea returned to its bed. God hurled the Egyptian army into the sea, so that the waters covered the chariots and horsemen, and Pharaoh's entire army. Not one of them survived.

But the Israelites marched through the sea on dry land, and the waters formed a wall to their right and to their left.

So God saved Israel from the Egyptians that day. And when the people saw the Egyptians lying dead on the shores of the sea and saw God's mighty power, they had faith in God and God's servant Moses.

Then Moses and the Israelites sang this song to God:

I will sing to God, for God has triumphed.
Horse and rider God has hurled into the sea!

Who is like You, O God, among the mighty?
Who is like You, great in holiness!

Then Miriam the prophet took a tambourine in her hand, and all the women followed her, dancing with their tambourines and drums.
Miriam chanted to them:

Sing to God, for God has triumphed—
Horse and rider God has hurled into the sea!

The Gifts of Manna and Quail

Exodus 16

In the middle of the second month after leaving Egypt, the Israelites began to grumble against Moses and Aaron.

They said, "If only we had died in Egypt! At least there we used to sit by the stew pots and eat bread until we were full! Instead you have brought us into this wilderness to starve to death!"

Then God said to Moses, "I will now rain bread from the skies, and the people will go out each day and gather their portions. And I will test them to see whether they will follow My instructions. On the sixth day of the week, the portions they gather will be double—since none will fall on the seventh day, for it is a day of rest."

Moses and Aaron said to the Israelites, "In the evening you will know that it was God who brought you out of Egypt, and in the morning you will see God's glory. For God has heard your complaints and will give you meat in the evening and bread in the morning. Why do you come to us to complain? It is really God you are complaining against!"

That evening, flocks of quail flew in and covered the camp. In the morning, dew blanketed the camp. When the dew melted, the desert was covered with white flakes, like frost. When the Israelites saw this, they said to one another, "*Man hu*? What *manner* of thing is this?" For they did not know what it was.

Moses said to them, "This is bread that God has given you to eat. Each day you are to gather only what you need, one measure per person, and one measure for each person in your tents."

The Israelites called this food manna. It was white like coriander seeds and tasted like honey.

And so the Israelites gathered the manna, some taking much, some taking little, but when they measured what they'd gathered, they discovered that every measure was exactly the same.

Moses said to them, "Do not leave any extra until morning."

But some of the Israelites ignored his warning and kept a portion overnight. But by morning, it was infested with maggots and stank. Moses was angry with them for disobeying God's command.

Every morning they gathered what they needed, and when the sun grew hot, the manna that was left melted away. On the sixth day, they gathered double portions.

Moses said to the leaders of the people, "Tomorrow is the holy Sabbath, a day of rest. Cook what you wish, and leave the rest until morning."

They did as Moses said, and the manna did not spoil by morning.

Moses said, "Today no manna will fall, for it is God's Sabbath. Six days you will gather it, but on the seventh day, the Sabbath, you will find none."

But some of the people did not believe Moses. So they went out on the Sabbath to gather their portions. But they found nothing.

God said to Moses, "How long will they refuse to follow My instructions? Since I have given you the Sabbath, I am also providing you with two days of food on the sixth day. Let them not leave their tents on the seventh day."

And so the people rested on the seventh day.

For the next 40 years, the Israelites ate manna for their food. And when they reached the border of the land of Canaan, the manna disappeared.

The Ten Commandments

Exodus 19:1–20:18

In the third month after the Israelites left Egypt, they entered the wilderness of Sinai. And the people camped before the mountain.

Moses went up to God, who called to him from Mount Sinai and said to him, "Tell the Children of Israel, 'You have seen what I did to the Egyptians, and how I carried you on eagles' wings and brought you close to Me. If you obey Me faithfully and keep My covenant, you will be My special treasure among all the peoples of the earth, a kingdom of priests and a holy nation.' Say these words to the Children of Israel."

Moses called the elders and told them all that God had commanded.

And all the people answered together: "All that God has said we will do!"

Then Moses brought the people's words back to God.

God said to Moses, "I will come to you in a thick cloud, so that the people will hear when I speak with you, and they will trust you forever. Now go to the people and warn them to stay pure and to wash their clothes, and to be ready for the third day, for on the third day I will come down, in the sight of all the people, to Mount Sinai. Tell the people, 'Beware of going up on the mountain or touching its borders. For whoever touches the mountain will die. Whether animal or human, they shall not live.' When the shofar sounds a long blast, then they may go up on the mountain."

Moses came down from the mountain and told the people all that God had commanded.

On the third day, as morning dawned, there was thunder and lightning, and a dense cloud, and a very loud blast of the shofar, and all the people in the camp trembled. Moses led the people out of the camp toward God, and they took their places at the foot of the mountain.

Mount Sinai was covered in smoke, for God had come down upon it in fire. The smoke rose like the smoke of a furnace, and the whole mountain shook violently. The blare of the shofar grew louder and louder. When Moses spoke, God answered him in thunder. God came down to the top of Mount Sinai, and Moses went up.

Then God spoke all these words:

※ *I the Lord am your God who brought you out of the land of Egypt, the house of slavery. You shall have no other gods besides Me.*

※ *You shall not make for yourselves a sculptured image, or anything resembling what is in the heavens above, or on the earth below, or in the waters under the earth. You shall not bow down to these idols or serve them.*

※ *You shall not swear falsely by God's name, for I will not pardon anyone who swears falsely by My name.*

※ *Remember the Sabbath day and keep it holy. Six days you shall do all your work, but the seventh day is My Sabbath. You shall not do any work—you, your son or your daughter, your male or your female slave, or your cattle, or the stranger who is within your gates. For in six days God made heaven and earth and sea, and all that is in them, and God rested on the seventh day. Therefore, God blessed the Sabbath day and made it holy.*

※ *Honor your father and your mother, so that you may live long on the land that the Lord your God is giving you.*

※ *You shall not murder.*

※ *You shall not commit adultery.*

※ *You shall not steal.*

※ *You shall not testify falsely against your neighbor.*

※ *You shall not covet your neighbor's house, or his wife, or his male or female slave, or his ox or his donkey, or anything that belongs to your neighbor.*

All the people saw the thunder and lightning, the blast of the shofar, and the mountain smoking. When the people saw all this, they backed away and stood at a distance.

They said to Moses, "You speak to us, and we will obey, but do not let God speak to us, or we will die."

Moses said to them, "Do not be afraid, for God has come only to test you and to be sure that you will always revere God, so that you do not go down the wrong path."

Then Moses approached the thick cloud where God was.

Moses remained on the mountain covered in cloud for 40 days and 40 nights.

The Golden Calf

Exodus 32

When the Israelites saw that Moses was not coming down from the mountain after so many days, the men came to Aaron and said to him, "Come, make us a god to lead us! For that man Moses, who brought us out of the land of Egypt—we don't know what's happened to him."

Aaron said to them, "Take the gold rings from the ears of your wives, your sons, and your daughters, and bring them to me."

And they did so. Aaron took the gold, melted it down, and shaped it into the figure of a calf.

The people cried: "This is your god, O Israel, who brought you out of the land of Egypt!"

Then Aaron built an altar and declared, "Tomorrow will be a festival to God."

Early the next day, the people offered sacrifices. Then they ate and drank and rose up to dance.

God said to Moses, "Hurry down the mountain! Your people, whom you brought out of Egypt, have disgraced themselves. They have been quick to turn away from the path I have commanded them to follow. They have made for themselves a golden calf and bowed down to it and sacrificed to it, saying, 'This is your god, O Israel, who brought you out of the land of Egypt.' What a stiff-necked people they are! Now leave Me, so that My anger can blaze against them and destroy them. And I will make of you a great nation."

But Moses said, "Do not let Your anger blaze against Your people, whom You redeemed from Egypt with great power and with a mighty hand. What if the Egyptians were to say, 'God took them out of Egypt only to destroy them in the mountains and wipe them from the face of the earth'? Turn away Your anger and reject Your plan to punish Your people. Remember Your servants Abraham, Isaac, and Jacob and Your promise to make their descendents as numerous as the stars of heaven and to give them the Promised Land forever."

So God held back from punishing the people.

Then Moses descended carrying the two Tablets of the Commandments, inscribed by God on both sides.

When Joshua heard the wild shouts of the people, he said to Moses, "There is a cry of war in the camp!"

But Moses replied, "No, it is not the chant of victory nor the chant of defeat that I hear, but rather the sound of singing."

As soon as Moses came near the camp and saw the golden calf and the people dancing, he became very angry. He hurled the tablets and shattered them at the foot of the mountain. Then he took the golden calf and burned it. He ground the gold into powder, scattered it over the water, and made the Israelites drink it.

Then Moses said to Aaron, "What did the people do to you to make you bring such great sin upon them?"

Aaron said, "Do not be angry, my lord! You know how bad this people can be. They said to me, 'Make us a god to lead us. For that man, Moses, who brought us out of the land of Egypt—we do not know what has happened to him.' So I said to them, 'Whoever has gold, take it off.' And they gave it to me and I threw it into the fire—and out came this calf!"

Moses saw that the people were out of control, and that Aaron had failed to control them.

Moses told the people, "You have been guilty of a great sin. But I will go back up the mountain and speak to God. Perhaps I will be able to clear away your sin."

So Moses went back up to God and said, "Alas, this people is guilty of a great sin in making themselves a god of gold. Please forgive them. But if you will not, then erase me from Your book!"

God said to Moses, "I will erase from My book only the person who has sinned against Me. Go lead the people where I told you to go. My angel will go before you. But when the time of judgment comes, I will hold them responsible for their sins."

Then God sent a plague among the people because of the golden calf that Aaron had made.

The Twelve Spies

Numbers 13–14

A few years after leaving Egypt, the Children of Israel reached the border of Canaan and camped there.

God said to Moses, "Send 12 men to scout out the land of Canaan, one from each tribe, each a leader among his people."

Moses said to the twelve scouts, "Go see what kind of land it is. Are the people who live there strong or weak, few or many? Is the land good or bad? Are the cities open or walled? Is the soil rich or poor? Are there trees or not? And be sure to bring back some of the fruit."

So they went to scout out the land, and they traveled through the Negev Desert and came to Hebron, where the giant Anakites lived. Now it happened that this was the season when the grapes were beginning to ripen.

When they reached an oasis, they cut down a single grape cluster that was so heavy that it took two men to carry it. They also collected pomegranates and figs.

After forty days, they returned to the Israelite camp.

Two of the scouts, Caleb and Joshua, brought back a positive report, confident that the Israelites could conquer the land.

But the majority of the scouts gave a negative report.

They said, "The people who live there are powerful and their cities are large and fortified. These people are stronger than we are—we cannot defeat them! The land swallows up those who settle there. The people living there are giants. We seemed like grasshoppers in our own eyes, and so we must have looked to them."

That night the people cried out, complaining to Moses and Aaron, "If only we had died in the land of Egypt! Or if only we could die here in this wilderness! Why is God bringing us to this land to die by the sword? Our wives and children will be taken captive. We were better off in Egypt!"

They said to each another, "Let's return to Egypt!"

Then Moses and Aaron flung themselves down on the ground before the people. Joshua and Caleb said to the people, "The land that we saw is a very, very good land, flowing with milk and honey. If God is pleased with us, God will bring us there and give this land to us. Only you must not rebel against God! Do not be afraid of the people of this land, for we will conquer them. God is with us—do not be afraid of them!"

But the people threatened to stone them.

Then God said to Moses, "How long will this people reject Me? How long will they have no faith in Me despite all the miracles that I have performed on their behalf? I will strike them down with a plague and disown them. I will make you into a nation even greater than they!"

But Moses said to God, "When the Egyptians hear that You have slaughtered this people, they will tell those who live in this land. And when the nations of this land learn that You have killed every one of Your people, they will say, 'God was not able to bring them into this land, so God killed them in the wilderness.' Show that You are indeed 'slow to anger, full of kindness, forgiving sin and wrongdoing.' Please forgive Your people out of Your great kindness, as You have forgiven them ever since Egypt."

God replied, "I will forgive them as you have asked. But not one of these men will see the land I promised to their ancestors. Out of the generation that left Egypt, only Caleb and Joshua will enter the land."

As for the ten scouts who brought back the evil report, they died of a plague.

Then God said to Moses and Aaron, "Say to the people, 'Your children will enter the land that you have rejected. But they will wander in the wilderness for 40 years, suffering on account of your sin, until every last one of you has dropped dead. Forty years will you be punished, one year for each day that you scouted the land. This way, you will learn what happens to those who reject Me.'"

When Moses told the people what God had said, they were filled with sorrow. Early the next morning, they marched toward the hill country of Canaan, saying, "We are now ready to go where God has commanded, for we were in the wrong."

But Moses said to them, "Why do you continue to disobey God? You will not succeed! Do not go into the land, for God is not with you. If you go, you will fall to the swords of the Amalekites and the Canaanites."

But they did not listen to Moses. They marched toward the hill country without either the Ark of the Covenant or Moses. And the Amalekites and the Canaanites defeated them, as Moses had predicted.

The Rebellion of Korah

Numbers 16

Now the Levite Korah—together with more than 250 respected leaders of the community—rebelled against Moses and Aaron.

They came to Moses and Aaron and said to them, "You two have gone too far! The whole community of Israel is holy, and God dwells among us. Why do you think you're better than the rest of us?"

When Moses heard this, he said to Korah, "By morning, God will show us who belongs to God and who is holy. Whoever God has chosen will be allowed to come near. So take fire pans for yourselves. Tomorrow put fire and incense in them and bring them before God. We will see whom God considers holy. You are the ones who have gone too far, sons of Levi!"

Moses went on, "Listen to me, sons of Levi. Is it not enough that the God of Israel has set you apart from the rest of the community, to bring you close through your work in the Tabernacle and through attending to the needs of the people? Do you also want to be priests like Aaron and his sons? It is not against Aaron but against God that you have rebelled!"

Moses then said to Korah, "Tomorrow you and your followers and Aaron will appear before God. Each man will take his fire pan and place incense upon it and offer it to God."

So the next day each man took his fire pan, put fire and incense upon it, and stood at the entrance to the Tent of Meeting before the whole community.

Then God said to Moses and Aaron, "Stand back so I can destroy them all in an instant!"

Moses and Aaron fell on their faces and said, "O God, if one man sins, will you condemn the whole community?"

God replied, "Tell the community: 'Move away from the tents of Korah and his followers.'"

So Moses said to the people: "Move away from the tents of these evil men, and do not touch anything that belongs to them, or you will be wiped out because of their sins."

And the people did as Moses instructed.

Then Moses said, "By this will you know that God, not my own heart, has directed me to do these things. If these men die ordinary deaths like other men, it was not God who sent me. But if God does something out of the ordinary, making the earth open its mouth and swallow up these men and everything that belongs to them, then you will know that these men have offended God."

Moses had barely finished speaking when the earth split open beneath Korah and his followers, swallowing them, their households, and all their possessions. Then the earth closed back over them so that they disappeared.

Moses Strikes the Rock

Numbers 20:1–13, 22–29

In the fortieth year after leaving Egypt, Miriam died while the Israelites were camped in the wilderness of Zin, and she was buried there.

Now the community had no water, and they rebelled against Moses and Aaron, saying, "Why did you bring us and our animals here to die in this wilderness? Why did you take us out of Egypt to bring us to this wicked place with no grain or figs or grapes or pomegranates, and no water to drink?"

Then God said to Moses, "Take your staff and gather the people—you and your brother, Aaron—and before their eyes, tell the rock to bring forth water for the community and its animals."

So Moses took his staff as he had been commanded, and he and Aaron gathered the people in front of the rock.

Moses said to them, "Listen, you rebels! Do you want us to bring forth water for you from this rock?"

Then Moses raised his hand and hit the rock twice with his staff, and water gushed out of the rock. The people and their animals drank.

God said to Moses and Aaron, "Because you did not trust Me enough to speak to the rock but struck it, you will not bring this people to the land I am giving to them."

Not long after this, Aaron died, and the priesthood passed to Aaron's son Eleazar. And the people mourned Aaron for 30 days.

Balaam and His Talking Donkey

Numbers 22:1–24:25

The Israelites came to Moab and camped on the Jordan River across from Jericho.

Then Balak, the king of Moab, sent messengers to the prophet Balaam. They said to him: "Out of Egypt comes a people who cover the face of the earth. Come put a curse on this people. Maybe then I can defeat them and drive them out of this land. For I know that those whom you bless are blessed, and those whom you curse are cursed."

Balaam said to them, "Stay here tonight. Tomorrow I will tell you what God says."

So they stayed with Balaam that night.

God came to Balaam and said, "Who are these people?"

Balaam replied, "King Balak of Moab sent them to me, saying, 'Out of Egypt comes a people who cover the face of the earth. Come put a curse on them. Then I may be able to drive them away.'"

God said to Balaam, "Do not go with them. You must not curse this people, for they are blessed."

In the morning, Balaam said to Balak's messengers, "Go home, for God will not let me go with you."

So they returned to Balak and told him that Balaam had refused to come.

Then Balak sent more messengers, even grander than the first.

They came to Balaam and said, "So says King Balak: 'Please do not refuse to come. I will give you a great reward and will do whatever you say. Only come and doom this people!'"

Balaam answered, "Even if Balak were to give me a house full of silver and gold, I cannot disobey the word of God. Stay here tonight and let me learn what God wants me to do."

That night God came to Balaam and said, "Go with these men. But you will do whatever I tell you."

The next morning, Balaam saddled his donkey and left with his two servants and the messengers from Moab. God was angry with Balaam for going, and sent an angel to stand in his way.

As Balaam was riding along, his donkey spotted the angel standing in the road, holding a sword in his hand. The donkey swerved from the path to avoid the angel and went into the field. Balaam beat her until she returned to the path.

Then the angel placed himself in a different part of the path, between two stone fences bordering two vineyards. When the donkey saw the angel, she pressed herself against one of the stone fences and crushed Balaam's foot. And he beat her again.

Once more the angel stood in the way, on a stretch of road so narrow that there was no room to move either to the left or right. When the donkey saw the angel, she collapsed under Balaam, and he beat her with his stick.

Then God opened the donkey's mouth, and she said to Balaam, "What have I done to make you beat me three times?"

Balaam answered, "You've made a jackass of me! If only I had a sword with me, I'd kill you!"

The donkey said to Balaam, "Am I not your donkey that you've been riding all along? Have I ever behaved this way before?"

Balaam replied, "No."

Then God opened Balaam's eyes so that he too saw the angel of God standing in the path with a sword in his hand. Balaam bowed down to the ground.

The angel said to him, "Why did you beat your donkey three times? It was I who stood in your way! When the donkey saw me, she turned aside three times. If she had not done so, I would have killed you and let her live."

Balaam said to the angel, "I acted wrongly because I did not know that you were standing in the way. If what I am doing displeases you, I will go back."

But the angel said to Balaam, "No, go with these men. But you must say only what God tells you to say."

So Balaam went with Balak's messengers.

Balak came out to meet Balaam.

Balak asked, "Why did you not come when I first invited you? Is there really no way for me to reward you?"

Balaam replied, "Can I say anything except what God puts in my mouth?"

The next day, Balak brought Balaam up to a high place, where he could see all the Israelites. There Balak built seven altars, as Balaam instructed him to do, and offered sacrifices upon each altar.

Then Balaam said to Balak, "Stay here by these sacrifices while I go off alone. Perhaps God will appear to me. If so, I will tell you what God reveals to me." And he went off by himself.

Then God appeared to Balaam and said to him, "Return to Balak and speak the words I tell you to say."

So Balaam returned to Balak and the princes of Moab, and proclaimed:

How can I curse those whom God has not cursed?
How can I doom those whom God has not doomed?
Who can number the Children of Israel,
As countless as grains of sand?

Then Balak said to Balaam, "What have you done to me? I brought you here to curse my enemies and instead you have blessed them!"

Balaam replied, "I can say only what God has put in my mouth."

Then Balak said, "Come with me to another place, where you can see only part of this people. There you can curse them."

But again Balaam spoke only words of blessing over Israel.

Then Balak said to him, "Neither curse nor bless them!"

But Balaam replied, "Whatever God tells me to do, that I must do."

So Balak took him to a third high place overlooking the wilderness. And when Balaam looked out over the tribes of Israel, the spirit of God came to him, and he said,

How beautiful are your tents, O Jacob!
Your dwelling places, O Israel!
Like palm groves that spread out,
Like gardens along a river.
Blessed are they who bless you.
Cursed are they who curse you.

Balak was furious with Balaam and said to him, "I called you here to curse my enemies, and instead you have blessed them three times! I was going to give you a rich reward, but God has denied you your reward. Go home!"

Balaam replied, "I told your messengers that no reward could make me say anything except what God commands me. I will now return home to my own people. But before I go, I will tell you that in days to come, Israel will conquer its enemies and triumph over its foes."

Then Balaam set off for home, and Balak went on his way.

Moses Says Good-Bye

Deuteronomy 31–34

Moses announced to all the Israelites: "I am now 120 years old. I can no longer remain active. God has said to me, 'You will not cross the Jordan River.' God will cross over ahead of you and will destroy the nations in your path. Joshua will be the one to lead you as God has said. Be strong and do not be afraid of these other nations, for God walks with you and will not desert you."

Then Moses called Joshua and said to him in front of the whole people, "Be strong, for you will bring this people into the land that God promised to their ancestors, and you will divide it among them. God will go before you and will be with you. Do not be afraid!"

Then Moses wrote down all the teachings of the Torah and gave them to the priests and to the sons of Levi, who carried the Ark of the Covenant, and to all the elders of Israel.

He said to them, "At the end of every seventh year, read this Torah aloud. Gather together the whole people—men, women, children, and the strangers who live among you—so that they can hear and learn to be faithful to God and all the words of this Torah. And their children, who have not known what you have known, will hear and will learn to honor God as long as they live in this land that you are now going to inherit on the other side of the Jordan."

And Moses said to the people, "Take these words to heart and tell your children to follow all the teachings of this Torah. For this Torah is your life. Follow its teachings, and you will live a long time in the land you are about to inherit."

Then God said to Moses, "Climb to the top of Mount Nebo and look out upon the land of Canaan, which I am giving to the Israelites. Upon this mountain you will die, as your brother, Aaron, died on Mount Hor."

Then Moses, the man of God, said good-bye to the people of Israel and blessed each of the Twelve Tribes. When he was done, he climbed to the top of Mount Nebo. There God showed him the whole land of Canaan.

God said to him, "This is the land that I promised to Abraham, Isaac, and Jacob and which I now give to your children. I have let you see it with your own eyes, but you will not enter it."

Then Moses, the servant of God, died in the land of Moab. God buried him there, and to this day no one knows his burial place. He was 120 years old when he died. His eyes were still sharp, and his strength still sound. And the Israelites mourned Moses for 30 days.

Then Joshua, the son of Nun, became the leader of the people. He was filled with the spirit of wisdom because Moses had laid his hands upon him. And the Israelites listened to him as God had commanded.

Never again did there arise in Israel a prophet like Moses, whom God knew face to face and who performed such wonders and miracles before Pharaoh in the land of Egypt, before the eyes of all Israel.

Joshua and the Battle of Jericho

Joshua 1–7

After the death of Moses, God said to Joshua: "My servant Moses is dead. Prepare to cross the Jordan with the people. For I am giving to you the land I promised to your ancestors. As I was with Moses, so will I be with you. Be strong and steady. I will not desert you. And you must not desert the Torah but must faithfully follow its teachings. Only then will you be successful."

When Joshua told the people all that God had commanded, they replied, "We will obey you just as we obeyed Moses!"

Then Joshua sent two spies to scout out the walled city of Jericho. That night they stayed with a woman of the city named Rahab, whose house was built into the city wall. When the king of Jericho was told that Israelite spies had come to Rahab's house, he sent his men to seize them.

But Rahab hid the two spies on the roof, under some stalks of flax.

She said to the king's men: "Yes, the men did come here, but I didn't know where they came from. They left after dark, just before the city gate was closed. I don't know where they went. If you go after them at once, you can catch them."

So the king's men rode off in the direction of the Jordan River. As soon as they were gone, the city gate was shut.

Then Rahab went up to the roof and said to the men she had hidden there, "I know that God has given this country into your hands. For we've heard how God dried up the Sea of Reeds when you left Egypt and what you did to your enemies on the way. All the inhabitants of this land are trembling before you. We've all lost heart. For your God is the only God in the heavens above and on the earth below. Since I've shown you kindness, swear to me in God's name that you'll show kindness to my family. Give me a sign that you'll spare the lives of my father and mother, my brothers and sisters, and their families."

The men replied, "We promise our lives for yours! If you keep our mission secret, we will show you true kindness when God gives us this land."

She said to them, "Go and hide in the hills for three days. When the king's men return to Jericho, then it will be safe for you to return to your camp."

They said to her, "Tie this crimson cord in your window and bring your father, your mother, your brothers, and all your family into your house. When we invade the country, we will guarantee the safety of everyone within your doors. But if anyone goes outside, or if you betray us, then the fault is yours. We will be released from our promise."

She replied, "So be it."

Rahab then lowered them down from the window by a crimson cord, for her house was built into the outer wall of the city. After they were gone, she tied the crimson cord in her window.

The men hid in the hills for three days, and the king's men did not find them. Then they returned to the Israelite camp and reported to Joshua all that had happened to them.

They said to him, "God has handed over this land to us, for everyone fears us."

Then the Israelites set out from their camp and stayed for three days on the banks of the Jordan.

Joshua commanded the people, "When you see the priests advancing with the Ark, follow behind it—but at a distance—and you will be shown the way, for you have never been this way before. Purify yourselves, for tomorrow God will perform wonders before you."

Then God said to Joshua, "Today, for the first time, I will raise you up in the eyes of Israel, so that everyone will know that I will be with you as I was with Moses."

Then Joshua said to the people, "Come closer and hear the words of God, so you will know that among you dwells a living God, who will drive out before you the nations of Canaan. Now choose 12 men, one from each tribe. When the priests carrying the Ark set foot in the Jordan River, the water will stop flowing and will rise up into a single mound."

Then the people set out, with the priests in the lead, carrying the Ark of the Covenant. And as soon as the priests' feet touched the water's edge, the waters piled up in a single mound, so that the water flowing down to the Dead Sea dried up. The priests carrying the Ark of the Covenant came to a standstill exactly in the middle of the Jordan, on dry land.

The people crossed over near the city of Jericho. And when the entire nation had finished crossing, God said to Joshua, "Tell the 12 men, one from each tribe, to pick up 12 stones from the riverbed where the priests are standing and to bring them to the place where you will spend the night."

The 12 men did as Joshua commanded. Joshua placed 12 other stones in the middle of the Jordan, at the exact spot where the priests had stood—and there they remain to this day.

And when all his instructions had been carried out, Joshua commanded the priests, "Come up out of the Jordan."

As soon as the priests' feet stepped onto the bank of the Jordan, the waters flowed back and resumed their course.

On the tenth day of the first month, the people crossed the Jordan and camped at the eastern border of Jericho. There Joshua set up the 12 stones that had been taken from the Jordan River.

Then Joshua said to the people, "One day when your children ask, 'What do these stones mean to you?' you will tell them, 'Here God dried up the waters of the Jordan while you crossed over on dry land, just as God did at the Sea of Reeds.' These stones will serve the Children of Israel as a reminder for all time."

And on the 14th day of the first month, the Israelites held the first Passover in their new land. The next day, they ate the produce of the land—matzah (unleavened bread) and parched grain. And on that day, the manna ended.

Now the walled city of Jericho was shut up tight against the Israelites. No one could leave or enter.

God said to Joshua, "I will now deliver Jericho into your hands. For six days, let all your troops complete one circuit around the city, with seven priests carrying seven shofars before the Ark. On the seventh day, march around the city seven times, with the priests blowing the shofars. And when you hear a long blast of the shofar, the people will utter a loud cry, and the city wall will collapse. Then the people will go forward."

And Joshua told the people what God had commanded.

For six days, they circled the city, making one circuit on each day. Seven priests marched before the Ark, blowing the shofars continuously. But the rest of the people remained silent, as Joshua had commanded them. Then they returned to the camp.

On the seventh day, they rose at dawn and marched around the city seven times. When they completed the seventh circuit, Joshua commanded the people, "Shout—for God has given you the city! But be careful not to take anything for yourselves. All the silver and gold and copper and iron is reserved for God. Spare only Rahab and all who are with her in her house, for she hid our scouts."

And so it happened. At the end of the seventh circuit around the city, the shofars sounded, and the people shouted. Then the walls of Jericho collapsed. The Israelites rushed into the city, and captured it.

Joshua sent the two spies to Rahab's house and they saved her and her family as they had promised. Rahab and her family lived among the Israelites—as they do to this day—because she hid the scouts who came to spy out Jericho.

God was with Joshua, and his fame spread throughout the land.

Deborah and Yael

Judges 4; 5:31

After Joshua died, the Israelites did what was evil in God's eyes. They rejected the God of their ancestors, who had brought them out of the land of Egypt, and instead bowed down to the gods of Canaan. God was angry with the people and let them fall into the hands of their enemies.

Then God heard the people's cries and felt pity for them. God raised up judges who saved them from their enemies. But the people did not listen to these judges, and continued to worship other gods.

Then God delivered the Israelites into the hands of Jabin, a Canaanite king. The commander of Jabin's armies was Sisera, who had 900 iron chariots. Sisera mistreated the Israelites cruelly for 20 years. And the Israelites cried out to God.

At that time, the prophet Deborah led Israel as a judge. She used to sit under a tree called the Palm of Deborah, and the people would come to her for judgment.

Deborah sent for the general Barak and said to him, "So commands the God of Israel: 'Take ten thousand men and march against Sisera's army. I will deliver Sisera with his chariots and soldiers into your hands.'"

But Barak replied, "Only if you go with me, will I go. If not, I will not go."

Deborah said, "I will go with you. But you will gain no honor, since God will deliver Sisera into a woman's hands."

Then Barak gathered ten thousand men, and Deborah went with him.

When Sisera heard that Barak's forces were marching against him, he ordered all his chariots and soldiers into battle.

Deborah said to Barak, "Go forward! For today God will give you victory!"

So Barak led his ten thousand men into battle.

God struck terror into the hearts of Sisera and his army when they saw Barak's army advancing toward them. Sisera leaped from his chariot and escaped the battlefield on foot.

He ran until he reached the tent of Yael, who greeted him and said, "Come in, my lord, and don't be afraid."

So Sisera came into Yael's tent, and she covered him with a blanket.

He said to her, "Please give me some water to drink, for I'm thirsty."

She gave him milk from a skin bag, and covered him again.

Sisera said, "Stand at the opening of the tent. If anyone comes by and asks you, 'Is there a man here?' tell him no."

Then Sisera lay down inside the tent and fell asleep. While he was sleeping, Yael took a tent stake and a mallet, crept up on him, and drove the stake through his forehead until it pierced the ground. And so Sisera died.

Then Barak came to Yael's tent, and Yael came out to meet him.

She said to him, "Come and I will show you the man you seek."

He went inside with her, and there lay Sisera, dead.

And the land was at peace for the next 40 years.

Gideon

Judges 6:1–7:25; 8:28

The Israelites again did what was evil in God's eyes, and God delivered them into the hands of the Midianites for seven years. The Israelites hid themselves in mountain caves, and the Midianites destroyed their harvests and their herds.

Then an angel of God came and sat down under an oak tree, which belonged to an Israelite named Joash. At that time, Joash's son Gideon was threshing wheat inside a winepress to hide it from the Midianites.

The angel appeared to Gideon and said, "God is with you, mighty warrior!"

Gideon replied, "Please, my lord, if God is really with us, why has all this happened to us? Where are all the miracles our elders told us about, saying, 'Did not God bring us up out of Egypt?' Why has God abandoned us and delivered us into Midian's hands?"

The angel said, "Go use your strength to save Israel from the Midianites. You are being sent as God's messenger."

"Please, my lord, how can I deliver Israel?" asked Gideon. "My clan is the humblest in the tribe of Manasseh, and I am the youngest in my father's house."

The angel said, "I will be with you, and you will defeat every last man in Midian."

"If I have truly gained favor in God's eyes," said Gideon, "then give me a sign that it is really God speaking to me. I will fetch a young goat and offer it to God."

So Gideon prepared a goat as an offering and baked unleavened bread from flour. He put the meat in a basket and poured broth into a pot, and he brought his offering to the angel under the oak tree.

The angel of God said to him, "Take the meat and the unleavened bread, put them on that rock, and spill out the broth."

Gideon did so.

Then the angel of God held out his staff and touched the meat and unleavened bread with it. A fire sprang up from the rock and burned up the meat and unleavened bread. Then the angel of God vanished from Gideon's sight.

"O my God," Gideon cried, "I have seen a divine angel face to face!"

That night God spoke to Gideon: "Pull down the altar of Baal belonging to your father, and build an altar to God in its place."

So that night Gideon took ten servants and did as God commanded him.

Early the next morning, the townspeople discovered that the altar of Baal had been torn down, and that a sacrifice had been offered on a newly built altar.

"Who did this?" they demanded to know. They soon learned that it had been done by Gideon, the son of Yoash.

The townspeople said to Yoash, "Bring out your son, for he must die! He has torn down the sacred altar of Baal."

Yoash said to them, "Does Baal need you to fight for him? Let him fight his own battles, because it is his altar that has been torn down."

Then the Midianites and their allies joined forces, crossed over the Jordan River, and camped near the place where Gideon lived.

Then the spirit of God filled Gideon. He sounded the shofar and sent messengers throughout the region, rallying all the men to join him to fight the enemy.

Gideon said to God, "If You really mean to save Israel through me, I will ask for another sign. I will place a wool fleece on the threshing floor. If dew falls only on the fleece but the ground remains dry, then I will know that You will save Israel through me, as You have said."

And so it happened. Early the next day, Gideon squeezed a bowlful of dew from the fleece, but the ground was dry.

Then Gideon said to God, "Do not be angry with me if I ask for one more test with the fleece. This time let only the fleece stay dry while dew wets the ground all around it."

That night God did as Gideon asked—the fleece stayed dry, but dew covered the ground all around it.

Early the next day, Gideon and all his troops set up their battle camp.

God said to Gideon, "You have too many men with you. When you defeat the Midianites, the Israelites might think, 'We have won by our own hands.' Therefore, announce to your men, 'Let anyone who is afraid go back home.'"

Twenty-two thousand men turned back, leaving ten thousand in the camp.

"There are still too many," God said to Gideon. "Take them down to the river, and I will thin them out there. I will tell you who will go with you and who will not go."

So Gideon took his troops down to the water.

God said, "Separate those who lap the water with their tongues like dogs from those who kneel down to drink."

Only 300 men lapped the water like dogs. The rest knelt down to drink.

God told Gideon: "With these 300 'lappers,' I will deliver Midian into your hands. Let the rest of the troops go home."

So the rest of the Israelites took their food and shofars and returned home, leaving only three hundred men to fight.

God said to Gideon, "Go attack the enemy camp, for I have delivered it into your hands. But if you are afraid to attack, sneak into the enemy camp with your servant and listen to what they say. After that, you will have the courage to attack."

That night Gideon and his servant slipped into the enemy camp, which stretched out over the plain like the sands of an endless shore. They eavesdropped at one of the tents. Gideon heard one man telling another man a dream he had had: "A loaf of barley was spinning through our camp like a whirlwind, and it struck one of the tents and flipped it over so that it collapsed."

The other man said, "This dream can mean only one thing—the sword of Gideon will soon defeat us in battle."

Then Gideon's heart filled with courage, and he returned to his camp. He called his soldiers, divided them into three columns, and gave each man a shofar and an empty jar with a torch in each jar.

He told them, "Watch me and do as I do. When I and the men with me get to the outskirts of the enemy camp and blow our horns, then blow your horns, too, and shout, 'For God and for Gideon!'"

When Gideon and the hundred men with him reached the outskirts of the enemy camp, they blew their shofars and smashed their jars. The rest of the troops did the same. Holding burning torches in their left hands and shofars in their right, they shouted, "A sword for God and for Gideon!"

The Midianites were so surprised to see their camp suddenly lit up and to hear the noise of so many blowing horns that they began attacking one another with their own swords and soon ran away in panic.

The Israelites chased after the Midianites and fought them until they were all defeated.

And the land was quiet for the next 40 years.

Samson

Judges 13–16

The Israelites again did what was evil in God's eyes, and God delivered them into the hands of the Philistines for forty years.

There was a certain man from the tribe of Dan whose name was Manoah. He and his wife had no children.

One day an angel appeared to the woman and said to her, "You will soon become pregnant and give birth to a son. Be careful not to drink any wine or liquor or eat anything impure. For your son will be a Nazirite, a person dedicated to God. No razor shall ever touch his head. And he will save Israel from the Philistines."

The woman went and told her husband, "A man of God came to me. He seemed like an angel of God! I didn't ask him where he came from, nor did he tell me his name. He told me that I would become pregnant and give birth to a son, who is to be a Nazirite from the day of his birth until the day he dies. That's why I'm not to drink wine or liquor or eat anything impure."

Manoah prayed to God, "Please send the man of God to us again, and let him teach us what to do with the child who will be born to us."

God listened to his prayer and sent the angel to the woman again while she sat alone in the field. She ran to tell her husband. Manoah followed his wife and came to the man of God.

Manoah asked him, "What is your name? For we would like to honor you when your words come true."

"You must not ask me my name," replied the angel, "for it is unknowable!"

Then Manoah offered a young goat and a grain offering as a sacrifice to God. And then a marvelous thing happened: As Manoah and his wife watched, the angel of God rose up toward heaven on the flames of the sacrifice. In terror, Manoah and his wife threw themselves to the ground. And the angel never appeared to them again.

Manoah said to his wife, "We will surely die, for we have seen a divine being."

His wife replied, "Had God meant to take our lives, God wouldn't have accepted our offering or let us see all these things or given us such wonderful news."

As the angel had promised, the woman soon became pregnant and gave birth to a son, whom she named Samson. The boy grew up, and God blessed him.

One day Samson saw a Philistine woman, and he went home and told his parents that he wished to marry her.

They said to him, "Is there no woman for you among our own people? Why must you go marry a Philistine?"

Samson answered, "She's the one who pleases me."

So Samson and his parents went to meet the woman's family. His parents did not know that this was all part of God's plan, for God wanted to anger the Philistines, who ruled Israel at this time.

When Samson reached the vineyards near where the woman lived, he was attacked by a full-grown lion. Filled with the spirit of God, Samson tore the lion apart with his bare hands—but he did not tell his parents what he'd done.

The following year, Samson went back to marry the Philistine woman. Along the way, he saw the carcass of the lion he had killed. Inside the animal's skeleton he found a swarm of bees and honey. He scooped up some of the honey with his hands and ate it on his way. When he met up with his parents, he gave them some of the honey to eat, but he did not tell them where he had gotten it.

Samson made a wedding feast, as young men used to do. The people of his wife's town chose 30 young men to celebrate with him.

Samson said to the young men, "I have a riddle for you. If you can solve it during the seven days of the wedding feast, I'll give you 30 linen robes. But if you can't guess the answer, then you must give me 30 linen robes."

"Let's hear your riddle," they replied.

He said to them:

"Out of the eater came something to eat,

Out of the strong came something sweet."

For three days they tried but could not guess the answer. On the fourth day, they said to Samson's wife, "Get the answer from your husband, or else we'll set your father's house on fire. Did you invite us here to ruin us?"

So Samson's wife came crying to him.

She said, "You don't really love me, Samson! You asked my fellow Philistines a riddle, but you won't tell me the answer."

"I haven't even told my own father and mother," Samson protested. "Why then should I tell you?"

For the next three days, she nagged him and cried many tears, until at last he told her the answer. She then told it to the townspeople.

On the seventh day, just before sunset, they said to Samson: "What is sweeter than honey and stronger than a lion?"

"If you hadn't gone to my wife," said Samson, "you would never have unriddled my riddle!"

Then Samson, ablaze with the spirit of God, went off and stripped 30 strangers of their robes, and gave the robes to the young men who had answered his riddle. Then, very angry about what had happened, he

returned home—but without his new wife. Her father then married her off to one of the wedding guests.

Some time later, during the wheat harvest, Samson came to visit his wife, bringing her a young goat as a gift.

He said to her father, "Let me go to my wife's room."

But her father would not let him go in.

He said to Samson, "I was so sure that you hated her that I married her off to one of the wedding guests. But she has an unmarried younger sister who is even more beautiful—marry her instead."

Samson replied, "Do not blame me for the harm I'm about to do to all you Philistines."

Then Samson went and caught 300 foxes. He bound their tails together, two by two, and tied a torch to each pair of tails. He then set the foxes loose among the Philistines' fields, scorching both the harvested and the standing grain, the vineyards and the olive trees.

"Who did this?" demanded the Philistines.

"It was Samson," they were told, "whose father-in-law gave his wife to one of his wedding guests."

And Samson went into hiding in a cave.

The Philistines then marched against Judah.

"Why have you gathered against us?" the men of Judah asked them.

"We've come to take Samson prisoner," they replied, "to pay him back for what he did to us."

Three thousand men of Judah then came to Samson in his cave.

They said to him, "You know that the Philistines rule over us. Why did you do this to us?"

"I did to them only what they had done to me," Samson replied.

They said, "We've come to take you prisoner and hand you over to the Philistines."

Samson said, "Then promise me you will not attack me yourselves."

They replied, "We promise that we'll only hand you over to them, but we will not kill you ourselves."

So they tied him up with two new ropes and took him to the Philistine camp.

When the Philistines saw Samson, they began to shout. Filled with the spirit of God, Samson ripped apart his bonds. Spotting the fresh jawbone of a donkey, he grabbed hold of it and with it killed a thousand men.

And Samson led Israel for the next 20 years.

Then Samson fell in love with a woman named Delilah. The lords of the Philistines came to her and said, "If you find out what makes Samson so strong and how we can overpower him and tie him up so that he's helpless, we'll each pay you eleven hundred shekels of silver."

So Delilah asked Samson, "Tell me, what makes you so strong? How can you be tied up so that you're helpless?"

Samson replied, "If I were tied up with seven branches from green saplings which haven't yet been dried for bowstrings, I would become as weak as any ordinary man."

So the Philistine lords brought Delilah seven branches from green saplings. She tied him up while the Philistines lay in ambush in the next room.

Then she called out, "Samson, the Philistines have come!"

Samson tore his bonds apart as if they were straw scorched by fire. And the secret of Samson's strength remained unknown.

Delilah said to him, "You lied to me, Samson! Tell me how you can be bound."

"If I were tied up with new ropes that have never been used," he told her, "I would become as weak as any ordinary man."

So Delilah tied him up with new ropes while the Philistines lay in ambush in the next room.

She cried, "Samson, the Philistines have come!"

But he snapped the ropes off his arms like thread.

Delilah said, "You've deceived me again! Now tell me how you can be bound."

Samson replied, "If you weave seven locks of my hair into your loom, and pin them to the wall, then I'll become as weak as any ordinary man."

She did so, but when she cried, "Samson, the Philistines have come!" he woke up and pulled himself free.

She said, "How can you say you love me if you won't trust me? You've now tricked me three times. Tell me what makes you so strong."

Samson was so tired of her nagging that he now told her everything.

He said, "No razor has ever touched my head, for I've been a Nazirite dedicated to God since I was born. If my hair were cut, my strength would leave me, and I would become as weak as any ordinary man."

Certain that this time Samson had told her the truth, Delilah sent a message to the lords of the Philistines: "Come once more, for this time he's told me everything."

So they came to her, bringing the money with them. After she had lulled Samson to sleep on her lap, she called for them to cut off the seven locks of his hair. Thus she weakened him, and his strength left him.

This time when she cried, "Samson, the Philistines have come!" he woke up and went to free himself as he had before, but God was no longer with him.

The Philistines seized Samson and blinded him. Then they took Samson, his feet bound in bronze shackles, down to the temple of their god, Dagon, and imprisoned him there as a mill slave, grinding grain.

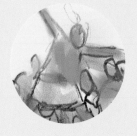

But Samson's hair soon began to grow back.

Now the lords of the Philistines gathered to celebrate and offer a great sacrifice to their god, Dagon.

When the people saw Samson, they sang:

Our god has delivered Samson—
The enemy who ruined our land
And killed so many of us—
Into our hands.

And the people cried, "Let Samson dance before us!"

So he danced for them.

Samson said to the boy who was leading him by the hand, "Let go of me. Let me lean upon the pillars that the temple rests upon."

Now the temple was filled with three thousand men and women on the roof, including all the lords of the Philistines. They all watched Samson dance.

Then Samson cried out to God, "O God, remember me! Give me strength just this once. Let me take revenge on the Philistines, if only for one of my two eyes!"

With his two arms, Samson now gripped the two middle pillars that the temple rested upon and cried, "Let me die with the Philistines!"

Then he pulled with all his might.

The temple came crashing down upon the lords of the Philistines and upon all the people. Those who died outnumbered those Samson had killed during his lifetime.

Samson's brothers and all his father's household came and carried him to the tomb where his father, Manoah, lay buried and buried him there.

Samson was a judge in Israel for 20 years.

Hannah's Prayer

1 Samuel 1:1–2:21

In the hill country of Ephraim lived a man named Elkanah, who had two wives. His wife Peninnah had many children, but his wife Hannah had none. Peninnah used to make fun of Hannah because she was childless, making Hannah so miserable that she cried and refused to eat.

Elkanah said to her, "Why are you so sad, Hannah? Am I not as good to you as 10 sons?"

Every year Elkanah and his family went up to Shiloh to offer sacrifices to God. One year, after they had eaten their meal at Shiloh, Hannah prayed to God. It so happened that the priest Eli was sitting nearby at the door to the temple.

Crying bitter tears, Hannah made this vow: "O God, if you will notice my suffering and remember me and give me a son, I'll dedicate him to Your service all the days of his life. I will never let a razor touch his head."

Eli watched Hannah's mouth as she prayed. Because Hannah was praying silently in her heart, her lips moved, but her voice could not be heard. Eli thought she was drunk and said to her, "How long will you stay drunk? Sober up!"

Hannah answered, "Oh, no, my lord! I'm not drunk. I'm just a bitter woman, pouring out her heart to God. Don't consider me sinful. It's only my sorrow speaking."

"Then go in peace," said Eli, "and may God answer your prayers."

"You've been most kind," answered Hannah.

Then she went and ate and was no longer sad.

Early the next morning, Eli and his family returned home.

God remembered Hannah, and she became pregnant and gave birth to a son, whom she named Samuel, *Shemu-el*, meaning "I asked God for him."

The following year, when Elkanah and his household went up to Shiloh to sacrifice to God, Hannah did not go with them.

She said to her husband, "I won't go to Shiloh with you until Samuel is weaned. For as soon as I bring him to the House of God, he must remain there forever."

"Do what you think is best," answered Elkanah.

So Hannah stayed home and nursed her son until he was weaned.

Then she took Samuel, along with an offering, to the House of God in Shiloh. The priests brought the boy and his mother to Eli.

Hannah said to Eli, "My lord, I'm the woman who once stood before you and prayed for this boy. God has granted my request. As I promised, I'm now lending my son back to God, for as long as he lives."

Then Hannah prayed:

God brings death and gives life,

God makes some poor and others rich;

God brings some down, and lifts others up.

God will judge the whole earth.

Then Elkanah and Hannah went home, without Samuel. And Samuel began to serve God under the priest Eli. Every year when Elkanah and his family came to Shiloh, Hannah brought Samuel a little robe she had made for him.

Eli blessed Hannah and Elkanah, saying, "May God give you more children to make up for the loan Hannah has made to God."

God again remembered Hannah, and she gave birth to three more sons and two daughters.

And Samuel grew up dedicated to serving God.

Samuel the Prophet

1 Samuel Chapters 3–7

One night Samuel lay sleeping near the Holy Ark. Eli the priest, who was now nearly blind, was sleeping in his usual place. The holy lamp had not yet gone out.

God called to Samuel, and the boy answered, "Here I am."

He ran to Eli and said, "Here I am. You called me."

Eli said, "No, I didn't call you. Go back to sleep."

So Samuel went back to his place and lay down.

God called again, "Samuel!"

Samuel went back to Eli and said, "Here I am. You called me."

But Eli said, "I didn't call you, my son. Go back to sleep."

Then God called to Samuel a third time.

Samuel went back to Eli and said, "Here I am. You called me."

Then Eli understood that God was calling the boy. He said to Samuel, "Go lie down. If you're called again, say, 'Speak, God, for Your servant is listening.'"

So Samuel returned to his place and lay down.

God again called to the boy, "Samuel! Samuel!"

Samuel answered, "Speak, God, for Your servant is listening."

God said to Samuel, "The time is coming when I will punish the priestly family of Eli and all his descendants. For his two sons have acted wickedly. They steal the best portion of every sacrifice brought to My altar. And Eli has done nothing about it. Because of their sins, Eli's family will be disgraced and their power destroyed."

The next morning Samuel was afraid to tell Eli what God had said to him. But Eli sent for him and said, "Samuel, my son."

Samuel answered, "Here I am."

Eli said, "What did God say to you? Keep nothing from me—not a single word."

So Samuel told Eli everything.

Eli said, "God will do what is right."

Samuel grew up, and God was with him. All of Israel knew that Samuel was a true prophet of God. Samuel's word spread throughout the land.

Then Israel went to war against the Philistines, and Israel was defeated.

The elders of Israel said, "Let us bring the Ark of the Covenant down from Shiloh. Then God will surely be with us and will save us from our enemies."

So Eli's two sons brought the Ark from Shiloh to the Israelite camp. When the people saw the Ark, they shouted so loudly that the earth echoed with the sound.

When the Philistines learned that the Ark had been brought into the Israelite camp, they were afraid.

They said, "God has come to their camp! Who will save us from this mighty God, who struck down the Egyptians with every kind of plague? Let's fight bravely, or we'll become slaves to the Hebrews!"

So the Philistines fought hard and again defeated Israel. They captured the Ark, and killed Eli's two sons.

A messenger came to Shiloh from the battlefield and found Eli sitting on a seat beside the road. Eli was now ninety-eight years old and blind.

The messenger told Eli, "The Philistines have defeated Israel. Your two sons are dead, and the Ark of God has been captured."

Hearing this news, Eli fell backward, broke his neck, and died. He had served Israel as a judge for forty years.

The Philistines brought the Ark to the temple of Dagon in Ashdod and placed it beside the statue of their god. The next day they found Dagon lying face down on the ground in front of the Ark. They stood the statue back up, but the next morning it was lying down again on the ground, this time with its head and hands chopped off.

Then God struck the people of Ashdod with a plague of boils. So they moved the Ark to Gath. But the people of Gath, too, were plagued with boils, and mice overran their fields. Then the Ark was moved to Ekron. But the people of Ekron likewise suffered with boils.

So the Philistines sent for their priests and fortune-tellers and asked them, "What should we do with this Ark? How can we send it back?"

The priests and fortune-tellers said, "If you wish to be healed, you must send it back with gifts. Don't harden your hearts like Pharaoh and the Egyptians. Instead, make five golden boils and five golden mice, representing the five lords of the Philistines. Then harness two young cows to a cart, and on this cart place the Ark as well as a chest containing the five golden boils and the five golden mice. Then let the cows find their own way. If they head toward the territory of the Israelites, we'll know that these plagues have been sent by God. But if they go some other way, we'll know that it's all happened by chance."

When they sent the cows on their way, the animals headed toward the territory of the Israelites, turning neither to the right nor the left. The Ark was brought to the house of Abinadab, where it remained for safekeeping.

When the Ark was once again in Israel, Samuel said to the people, "Get rid of all your foreign gods and serve God alone. God will then save you from the hands of the Philistines."

So the people got rid of their foreign gods. They fasted and confessed their sins.

The next time the Philistines attacked Israel, Samuel cried out to God on behalf of the people. God thundered against the Philistines so that they panicked and ran away. God protected Israel from the Philistines as long as Samuel lived.

And the Ark of God remained in the house of Abinadab for 20 years.

Israel's First King

1 Samuel 8:1–10:25

When Samuel was old, he appointed his two sons as judges. But they did not follow their father's honest ways. Instead they accepted bribes and acted unfairly.

Then the elders of Israel came to Samuel and said to him, "You are old, and your sons do not follow your ways. Appoint a king to rule over us, like all the other nations."

Their words upset Samuel, and he prayed to God.

God said, "It is not you but Me they have rejected as their king. They now turn away from Me as they have done ever since I brought them out of Egypt. Listen to their demands, Samuel, but warn them what such a king will do to them when he rules over them."

So Samuel told the people what God had said, warning them, "A king will take away your sons for his army and will keep them many years. He will make them tend his fields and make weapons for his wars. He will take away your daughters to serve him as perfumers, cooks, and bakers. He will give away your fields, vineyards, and olive groves to his favorites and will tax you to support his royal court. He will demand that you hand over to him your slaves and your herds. And the day will come when you cry out because of this king you've chosen—and God will not answer you."

But the people would not listen to Samuel.

They demanded, "Give us a king so we can be a nation like all other nations. Let our king rule over us and lead us into battle."

And God said to Samuel, "Do as they wish."

In the tribe of Benjamin lived a man named Kish, whose son Saul was the most handsome man among the Israelites, standing a head taller than any other man.

God told Samuel, "Tomorrow I will send you a man whom you will anoint king over Israel. He will save My people from the hand of the Philistines, for I have heard their cries."

Two days before Kish's donkeys had wandered off, and he sent his son Saul and a servant to look for them. The two men traveled throughout the territory but could not find them.

Saul said to his servant, "Let's turn back or my father will start worrying about us instead of the donkeys."

The servant replied, "There is a man of God nearby, a prophet, whose words always come true. Maybe he can help us with our errand."

Saul asked, "What gift can we bring to this man of God? Our bags are empty."

The servant said, "I have a quarter shekel of silver."

So they went to the town where Samuel lived and met him at the town gate.

As soon as Samuel saw Saul, God said to him, "This is the man!"

Saul asked Samuel, "Where is the house of the prophet?"

Samuel said, "I am that prophet. Go to the altar, for you will eat with me today. Tomorrow morning we will talk about what's on your mind. As for the donkeys that wandered off three days ago, do not worry about them, for they have been found. As for you, all Israel has been waiting for you!"

That night Samuel hosted a meal for Saul, his servant, and 30 other guests. The next morning, as he was leading Saul and his servant out of town, Samuel said to Saul, "Send your servant ahead. For now I will make known to you the word of God."

Samuel took a jug of olive oil and poured some on Saul's head. He kissed him and said, "God is anointing you king over Israel. When you leave me today, you will meet two men near Rachel's tomb. They will tell you that your father's donkeys have been found and that your father is worried about you. Then go to the oak tree near Tabor where you will meet three men making a pilgrimage to Bethel. One will be carrying three young goats, another three loaves of bread, and the third a jar of wine. They will greet you and offer you two loaves of bread. You will then go to the Hill of God, where you will meet a band of prophets playing harps, tambourines, and flutes. The spirit of God will seize you, and you will join them. Once you have seen all these signs, you will know what to do, for God is with you. You should then go to Gilgal and wait for me for seven days. Then I will tell you what to do next."

So Saul went on his way with a lighter heart. And all the signs came to pass as Samuel had predicted.

When Saul returned home, he told his family all that Samuel had predicted about finding the donkeys, but he did not reveal to them that Samuel had anointed him king.

Then Samuel gathered the people together and drew lots to see who would become Israel's king. The lot fell upon Saul.

The people proclaimed, "Long live the king!"

So Saul was crowned king at Gilgal.

But in time God came to regret choosing Saul as king, for Saul disobeyed God's commands. So God rejected Saul and tore the kingship from him. Then God chose someone more worthy to rule Israel.

David and Goliath

1 Samuel Chapters 15–17

After Saul was rejected as king, God sent Samuel to Bethlehem to anoint the boy David, the eighth and youngest son of Jesse, as the future king over Israel.

Then the spirit of God deserted Saul, and he was gripped by an evil spirit, which overpowered him from time to time. The king was told about a handsome and brave young shepherd who was skilled at playing the harp. And so David entered Saul's service to play music to calm his troubled king.

The Philistines again went to war against Israel. The two armies lined up against each other on facing hills, with a ravine between them. Then the champion of the Philistines stepped forward—Goliath of Gath, a giant of a man who stood over nine feet tall. He wore heavy bronze armor—helmet, breastplate, leg guards, and shield—and carried an iron-tipped javelin slung over his shoulder.

Goliath called out to the Israelites, "Why should you all fight? Send out your own champion to fight against me. If he kills me, we'll be your slaves. But if I kill him, you'll be our slaves and serve us. I defy you, Israelites! Choose one man and let us fight!"

When Saul and his army heard the Philistine's challenge, they were struck with fear. For the next forty days, each morning and each evening, Goliath dared the Israelites to send a champion to fight him, but none came forward.

David's three oldest brothers were soldiers in Saul's army. One day Jesse said to his youngest son, David, "Take this roasted corn and these loaves of bread to your brothers in Saul's camp. See how your brothers are doing and bring back a report to me."

David set out early the next morning and reached the Israelite camp just as the two armies were lining up against each other as they did each day.

While David was talking with his brothers, Goliath stepped forward and shouted out his daily challenge.

David asked, "What will be done for the Israelite who kills that man? Who does that Philistine think he is to defy the army of God!"

The soldiers answered, "The king will reward such a man with great riches and the hand of his daughter in marriage. And his family will never have to pay the king's taxes."

David's oldest brother, Eliav, overheard this conversation.

He said to David, "Why did you come here? Who's guarding our flock? You came only to watch the fighting!"

David said, "Why do you accuse me like this? I'm only asking questions!"

David continued to ask questions until the king heard about it. He sent for David.

David told Saul, "I will go and fight that Philistine!"

Saul said, "You cannot fight him. You are only a boy, and he has been a warrior all his life."

David said, "When I was a boy tending my father's flock, a lion or bear would sometimes carry off a sheep. I fought these wild beasts with my bare hands and rescued the sheep from their jaws. If an animal attacked me, I would seize it and kill it. I have killed both lions and bears. This Philistine will meet the same fate. God who has saved me from lions and bears will also save me from this Philistine."

Saul said, "Then go and may God be with you!"

Saul dressed David in his own battle armor—bronze helmet, breastplate, sword, and shield. But David could hardly walk in the heavy armor, so he took it off. Then he took his shepherd's staff, picked up a few smooth stones, and put them in his shepherd's pouch. Sling in hand, he walked toward the Philistine giant.

When Goliath saw David, he made fun of him, for David was only a boy.

"Am I a dog that you come against me with sticks? Come closer, and I'll feed your flesh to the birds of the sky and the beasts of the field!"

David answered, "You come against me with sword and spear and javelin, but I come against you in the name of the God of Israel, whom you have defied. Today God will deliver you into my hands. I will kill you and cut off your head. Then the whole land will know that there is a God in Israel."

Furious, Goliath charged toward him. David ran forward, scooped up a stone from his pouch, placed it in his slingshot, and hurled it at Goliath. The stone struck the Philistine in the forehead, and he crashed to the ground. David grabbed hold of Goliath's sword and cut off his head.

When the Philistines saw that their champion was dead, they fled in terror. The Israelite soldiers shouted out a war cry and chased after the Philistines, cutting down many of them with their swords.

Then David brought the head of Goliath to King Saul, and Saul gave David his daughter Michal in marriage as he had promised.

King Saul and the Witch of Endor

1 Samuel 24–25; 28:3–25; 31:1–6

David won many battles as the head of Israel's army. When he returned home after a victory, the women of Israel would greet him with singing and dancing. They chanted, "Saul has killed thousands, but David has killed tens of thousands."

King Saul became jealous of David and several times tried to kill him. But Saul soon regretted his anger and welcomed David back in peace. Again and again, Saul turned against David. Each time David had to flee for his life, hiding in the caves, forests, and hills of Judah. And Saul's son Jonathan, who loved David, helped him escape his father's rage.

After a time, David fled to the land of the Philistines, where he stayed for over a year.

The Philistines again went to war against Israel. Seeing how strong they were, Saul was filled with fear. He asked God for advice, but God did not answer him.

Saul commanded his attendants, "Find me a woman who talks with ghosts."

So they told him about a woman in Endor who talked with ghosts.

Now Saul had forbidden any Israelite from contacting ghosts or spirits. So he had to disguise himself when he set out with his two men. They came to the woman at night.

Saul said to her, "Call up a ghost whom I shall name."

The woman protested, "Don't you know that King Saul has forbidden such things? Why are you laying a trap for me! You will get me killed!"

Saul said, "I promise you will not get into trouble."

She asked, "Whom shall I call up from the dead?"

Saul replied, "Bring up Samuel."

When the woman saw the spirit of Samuel, she cried, "You have tricked me. You are King Saul!"

"Do not be afraid," replied Saul. "Tell me what you see."

She said, "I see a divine being rising from the earth."

Saul asked, "What does he look like?"

She answered, "An old man wrapped in a robe."

Then Saul knew that it was Samuel, and he bowed before him.

Samuel demanded, "Why have you disturbed me and brought me up from the grave?"

Saul replied, "I am in great trouble. The Philistines are attacking Israel, and God has turned away from me. I have called you up to ask you what I should do."

Samuel said, "Why do you ask me? God has become your enemy. As I predicted, the kingship has been ripped from your hands and has been given to David because you did not obey God's commands. God will now deliver Israel into the hands of the Philistines. And tomorrow you and your sons will be here with me."

And so it happened as Samuel had prophesied. The next day Saul and his sons were killed in battle, and David bitterly mourned their deaths.

David Conquers Jerusalem

2 Samuel Chapters 1–6

David was anointed king in Hebron and ruled over the House of Judah. But the people from Saul's tribe of Benjamin anointed their own king, Saul's son Ishboshet. Civil war raged between the two kingdoms for two years. Then Ishboshet was killed, and David was declared king over all of Israel.

David was thirty years old when he became king. He ruled in Hebron for seven and a half years.

Then David set out to conquer Jerusalem, which was inhabited at that time by the Jebusites. David defeated the Jebusites. To their stronghold, Zion, he gave a new name: the City of David. David's ally in the north, King Hiram, sent cedar beams, carpenters, and stonemasons to David, and they built a palace for the king in the City of David.

By this time David had three wives, Michal, Abigail, and Ahinoam, and six sons. David now took more wives, who gave him more sons and daughters.

When the Philistines heard that David had become king over Israel, they went to war against him. But David defeated them and drove them out of Israel.

David now gathered thirty thousand men, and they journeyed to the House of Abinadab, where the Ark of God had rested for 20 years. David and all the people escorted the Ark, dancing to the sounds of flutes, harps, tambourines, and cymbals. And they brought the Ark to David's new capital city of Jerusalem.

David set up the Ark inside a special tent. He blessed the people and gave every man and woman a loaf of bread and a raisin cake. Then the people returned to their homes.

David and Bathsheba

2 Samuel 11:1–12:25

During the season when kings went to war, David sent out his army to wage war against Israel's enemies. But David remained in Jerusalem. One afternoon as he was strolling on the palace roof, he saw a beautiful woman bathing. He sent someone to find out about her.

The messenger reported, "She is Bathsheba, the wife of Uriah the Hittite."

David sent for her and she came to the palace. She stayed with him, and then went back home.

She soon sent word to David, "I am pregnant with your child."

David then sent a message to his general Joab at the front: "Send Uriah to me."

When Uriah came before David, the king asked him, "How is the war going and how are the troops faring?" Then he said to Uriah, "Return home."

After Uriah left the palace, David sent a gift to his house.

But Uriah did not go to his house as the king had commanded. Instead he lay down to sleep at the entrance to the palace, along with the other officers. When David was told of this, he said to Uriah, "Why did you not go home?"

Uriah replied, "While the Ark and the people of Israel are far from home, and your majesty's army is camping on the battlefield, how can I go home and eat and drink and be with my wife?"

David said to Uriah, "Stay here one more day, and tomorrow I will send you back to the battlefield."

So Uriah stayed in Jerusalem another day. The next day, David sent for him. The king ate and drank with him until Uriah was drunk. But Uriah still did not go home but again went to sleep at the entrance to the palace with the officers.

The next morning, David wrote a letter to his general Joab: "Send Uriah to the front line, where the fighting is fiercest, so that he will be killed."

Joab placed Uriah in the front line, within range of the most skilled enemy archers. When the enemy attacked the Israelite army, several of David's officers were killed, among them Uriah.

Joab sent a messenger to David with a full report of the battle. He told the messenger, "When you report to the king, he may become angry at you and ask, 'Why did you come so near to the enemy city when you attacked it? Did you not realize that the enemy would shoot at you from the city walls?' Then say to the king, 'Your servant Uriah was among those killed.'"

The messenger went to David and repeated Joab's words to him. He told the king, "First the enemy attacked us in the open. We drove them back to their city gate. But the archers shot at us from the wall, and some of your officers fell, among them Uriah."

David said to him, "Give Joab this message: 'Do not be upset about what happened. War always takes its toll. Keep up the fighting and destroy the city!'"

When Uriah's wife heard that her husband was dead, she mourned him. When the mourning period was over, David sent for her. She became his wife and bore him a son.

God was unhappy with what David had done and sent the prophet Nathan to speak with him. Nathan told David the following story:

"There once were two men who lived in the same city, one rich and the other poor. The rich man had many flocks and herds, but the poor man had only one little lamb. The poor man took care of her, and she grew up together with him and his children. She shared his bread, drank from his cup, and snuggled on his chest. She was like a daughter to him.

"One day a traveler came to the rich man's house. But the rich man did not want to take an animal from his own flock to serve to his guest. So instead he took the poor man's lamb, slaughtered it, and served it to the traveler."

When David heard this, he became very angry. He said to Nathan, "The man who did this deserves to die! He must pay four times what the lamb was worth, because he showed no pity."

Nathan said to David, "You are that man! The God of Israel declares to you, 'I anointed you king and saved you from the hand of Saul. I gave you your master's house and your master's wives, and the House of Israel and Judah. And I would have given you twice as much if you were still not satisfied. Why then have you disobeyed and disappointed Me? You took the wife of Uriah and had him killed by the enemy's sword. Therefore, the sword will never depart from your house. I will bring you trouble from within your house. I will give your wives to another man before your very eyes. You acted in secret, but I will do all this in broad daylight before the entire people of Israel.'"

David cried, "I stand guilty before God!"

Nathan said, "God has pardoned your sin. You will not die. But because you rebelled against God, your newborn child will die."

Then Nathan went home.

The next day, the baby grew deathly ill, and on the seventh day, he died.

David comforted his wife Bathsheba over the loss of their son. She soon became pregnant again and gave birth to another son, whom she named Solomon.

David reigned over Israel for forty years. As Nathan had predicted, his reign was full of trouble. David named Solomon as king to rule after him, as he had promised Solomon's mother, Bathsheba.

The Wisdom of Solomon

1 Kings 3:5–28; 5:9–14; 9:1–9; 10:1–13

One night God appeared to Solomon in a dream and said, "Ask for whatever you wish, and I will give it to you."

Solomon said, "I am only a young boy with no experience as a leader. Please give me an understanding mind so that I will know the difference between right and wrong. For without such understanding, how can I judge this great people of Yours?"

God was pleased with Solomon's words and said to him, "Because you asked for wisdom—instead of long life, riches, or glory in battle—I now give you an understanding mind. There has never been nor will there ever be anyone as wise as you. And though you did not ask for riches and glory, I will give you these as well. And I will also grant you long life—if you walk in My ways and follow My commandments, as your father David did before you."

One day two women came to the king to ask his judgment.

The first woman said, "My lord, this woman and I live in the same house. I recently gave birth to a child. Three days later, she, too, gave birth to a child. Her son died because she rolled over on it. That same night, she took my baby from my side, and laid him down beside her. She laid down her own dead baby next to me. When I woke up the next morning to nurse my son, I saw that he was dead, but when I looked more closely in the morning light, I saw that the baby wasn't mine."

"No, the living son is mine," cried the other woman, "and the dead one is yours!"

The first woman replied, "No, the dead boy is yours. Mine is the living one!"

And they went on arguing before the king.

Solomon ordered that a sword be brought to him.

He said to his attendant, "Cut the living child in two. Give half to one woman and half to the other."

The first woman cried, "Please, my lord, give her the living child—only do not kill him!"

The other said, "No, cut him in two! He will be neither yours nor mine."

Solomon said to his attendant, "Do not put the child to death. Give him to the first woman, for she is his true mother."

When all of Israel heard about the king's judgment, they were amazed, for they saw that his wisdom truly came from God.

Solomon was wiser than anyone on earth, and his fame spread throughout the nations. He wrote three thousand wise sayings and more than a thousand songs. He knew all about trees and plants, beasts, birds, creeping things, and fishes. From all over the world people came to Jerusalem to hear Solomon's wisdom.

The Queen of Sheba came from her faraway kingdom to test Solomon with riddles. She traveled in a great caravan, with many camels carrying spices, gold, and precious stones. She asked Solomon many puzzling questions, and he answered them all.

When the Queen of Sheba saw how wise Solomon was and how marvelous was the great palace that he had built, the food and wines at his table, the pageantry of his court, and the sacrifices he offered in the House of God, she was breathless.

She said, "Everything that I heard in my country about your wisdom is true. I did not believe it until I came and saw with my own eyes. How lucky are those who serve you and can always hear your wisdom. Blessed is your God who set you on the throne of Israel, to rule with justice and righteousness."

The queen presented Solomon with great treasures: heaps of gold and spices and precious stones. Never again did Solomon receive such rich treasure. And Solomon gave the Queen of Sheba anything that her heart desired—and more.

Then she and her court returned to their own land.

Elijah and the Priests of Baal

1 Kings 17–18

Ahab became king over Israel and ruled the northern kingdom for twenty-two years. Ahab and his foreign wife Jezebel offended God by worshiping the Canaanite gods Baal and Asherah. Ahab did more to anger God than all the Israelite kings who came before him.

And the Prophet Elijah asked God to bring a drought because of the king's wickedness. Fearing for his life, Elijah fled to the land east of the Jordan and hid in the wilderness. There the ravens fed him at God's command. Then Elijah returned to Israel and took refuge with a poor widow. While he was with her, he performed miracles for her, increasing her supplies of flour and olive oil and bringing her son back to life after he died.

In the third year of the drought, God said to Elijah, "Go appear before Ahab. Then I will send rain upon the earth."

So Elijah set out to appear before the king.

When Ahab saw Elijah, he asked him, "Is that you, troubler of Israel?"

Elijah replied, "It is you, not I, who have troubled Israel. You have turned away from God's commandments and worshiped Baal. Now gather together all of Israel on Mount Carmel, together with the 450 prophets of Baal and the 400 prophets of Asherah who eat at Jezebel's table."

And Ahab did so.

Elijah asked the people who were gathered at Mount Carmel, "How long will you remain undecided? If the God of Israel is the true God, then that is whom you should follow. But if it is Baal, then follow him!"

But the people were silent.

Elijah said, "I am the only one of God's prophets left. But Baal has 450 prophets. Let two bulls be brought here, one for Baal and one for God. Let the priests of Baal choose one bull, cut it up, and lay it on the wood of the altar. But let no fire be lit. I will do the same with the other bull. We will then each call our God by name. The One who answers, that one is God."

Elijah said to the priests of Baal, "Prepare your bull first, because you are the majority."

So they took the bull, prepared it as an offering, and laid it on the altar. Then they called upon Baal from morning until noon, shouting, "Baal, answer us!"

But there was no answer.

Then they danced and leaped around the altar, but no answer came.

Elijah mocked them: "Shout louder! Maybe Baal is talking or is delayed. Maybe he is on a journey or asleep. You need to wake him up."

So they shouted louder and cut themselves, as was their custom. They kept shouting all afternoon, but still no one responded.

Then Elijah said to the people, "Come closer."

And they drew near.

Then Elijah repaired the ruined altar of God, using 12 stones, one for each tribe. Around the altar he dug a deep trench. Then he arranged wood on the altar, and upon the wood laid the bull he had cut up.

Elijah commanded, "Fill four jars with water and pour it over the bull and the wood."

He ordered this to be done three times. The water ran down the altar and filled the trench.

Then Elijah cried out, "God of Abraham, Isaac, and Jacob, let it be known today that You are the God of Israel, and I am Your servant. Answer me, O God, answer me!"

And God's fire came down and burned up the bull, the wood, and the stones, even licking up all the water in the trench.

When the people saw this, they threw themselves upon the ground and shouted, "Adonai is God! Adonai is God!"

Elijah cried, "Seize the prophets of Baal! Do not let even one of them escape!"

And all the prophets of Baal were put to death that day.

Then Elijah said to Ahab, "Go eat and drink, for I hear thunder."

And Ahab did so.

Elijah climbed to the top of Mount Carmel and crouched on the ground.

He said to his servant, "Look toward the sea. What do you see?"

The servant replied, "There is nothing."

Elijah sent him back seven times to look.

The seventh time the servant reported, "I see a cloud as small as a man's hand rising in the west."

Elijah sent word to Ahab, "Mount your chariot and be on your way, before the rain stops you."

For the sky was growing black with clouds, and a wind was rising. Then a heavy downpour rained down upon the earth. Ahab hitched up his chariot, and drove off.

Elijah gathered up the hem of his robe and ran in the rain all the way down the mountain.

The Still, Small Voice

1 Kings 19:1–21; 2 Kings 1–18

When Ahab told Jezebel what Elijah had done, how he had killed all the priests of Baal, she sent a messenger to Elijah, saying, "May the gods kill me if I have not made you like those you have killed by this time tomorrow."

Elijah ran for his life to the land of Judah, and went a day's journey into the wilderness. Exhausted, he sat down under a bush and prayed, "Enough, O God! Take my life."

Then he fell asleep under the bush. Suddenly an angel touched him and said, "Rise up and eat."

There beside his head was a cake baked on hot stones and a jar of water. He ate and drank and then lay down again.

Again the angel of God touched him and said, "Rise up and eat, or the journey will prove too much for you."

Elijah did so. He walked 40 days and 40 nights until he came to the Mountain of God at Horeb. He went into a cave and spent the night there.

The word of God came to him, saying, "Why are you here, Elijah?"

Elijah replied, "I have been a champion for God because the Israelites have broken Your covenant, torn down Your altars, and killed Your prophets. I alone am left, and the people want to kill me."

God said, "Come out and stand on the mountain before Me."

As Elijah stood on the mountain, God passed by.

First there was a great and mighty wind, splitting mountains and shattering rocks, but God was not in the wind.

After the wind, there was an earthquake, but God was not in the earthquake.

After the earthquake came a fire, but God was not in the fire.

And after the fire, came a still, small voice.

When Elijah heard this soft voice, he wrapped his cape around his head and stood at the mouth of the cave.

The voice said, "Why are you here, Elijah?"

Elijah replied, "I have been a champion for God because the Israelites have broken Your covenant, and now they want to kill me."

God said to him, "Go back the way you came. Go to Elisha, who will succeed you as My prophet."

So Elijah went to Elisha and found him plowing a field with 12 oxen. Elijah threw his cape over him.

Elisha said, "Let me kiss my father and mother good-bye, and then I will follow you."

Elisha followed after Elijah and became his disciple. Years later, when Elijah was finally taken from the world, carried off to heaven in a fiery chariot drawn by horses of fire, Elisha picked up Elijah's fallen cloak, and became a prophet in Israel.

Elisha and the Shunammite Woman

2 Kings 4:1–37

One day the prophet Elisha visited the town of Shunem. A rich woman lived there, and she begged him to stay for a meal. From then on, whenever he passed by, he would stop there to eat.

The woman said to her husband, "I am sure this is a holy man of God who always comes this way. Let's make a small room for him upstairs and furnish it with a bed, a table, a chair, and a lamp, so he can stay here whenever he comes to visit us."

One day Elisha came by, went upstairs, and lay down to rest.

Elisha asked his servant, Gehazi, "What can be done for this Shunammite woman? She has gone to all this trouble for us. Can we speak on her behalf to the king or the commander of the army?"

Gehazi replied, "The fact is that she has no son, and her husband is old."

Elisha said to the woman, "At this time next year, you will be cradling a son."

She said, "Please, my lord, you are a man of God. Do not lie to me!"

At this same time the following year, the woman gave birth to a son, as Elisha had foretold.

And the child grew up. One day, he went out to his father among the reapers in the field. Suddenly he cried to his father, "Oh, my head, my head!" And he fell to the ground.

His father called to a servant, "Carry him to his mother."

The servant picked up the boy and brought him to the house. The child sat on his mother's lap until noon, and then he died. His mother carried him upstairs and laid him on Elisha's bed. She closed the door and left him there.

Then she called to her husband, "Send me one of our servants and one of the donkeys, so I can travel quickly to the man of God and return home."

When the donkey was saddled, she said to her servant, "Hurry the beast along! Do not slow down unless I tell you."

She came to Elisha on Mount Carmel. When the prophet saw her coming from a distance, he said to his servant, Gehazi, "There is that Shunammite woman. Run to her and ask her, 'How are you? How is your husband? How is the child?'"

And Gehazi did so.

The woman said to Gehazi, "We are well."

But when she came to Elisha on the mountain, she grabbed hold of the prophet's feet. Gehazi was about to push her away, but Elisha said, "Leave her alone, for she is greatly distressed. But God has hidden from me the cause of her distress."

She said to Elisha, "Did I ask you for a son? Didn't I say, 'Do not lie to me!'"

Elisha said to Gehazi, "Dress yourself for a journey, take my staff in your hand, and go with her. If you meet anyone on the way, do not greet him, and if anyone greets you, do not answer him. Place my staff on the face of the dead boy."

But the boy's mother said, "I will not leave without you!"

So Elisha stood up and followed her.

Elisha came into the house and went upstairs. There on the bed lay the boy, dead. Elisha came into the room, shut the door, and prayed to God.

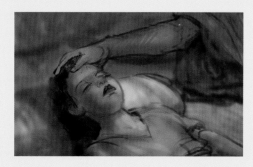

Then he climbed onto the bed and laid his body over the child's. He put his mouth on the boy's mouth, his eyes on his eyes, and his hands on his hands. The boy's body grew warm.

Then Elisha climbed down from the bed, walked once up and back across the room, then climbed back up on the bed and bent over the boy. The boy sneezed seven times, then opened his eyes.

Elisha said to Gehazi, "Call the Shunammite woman."

When she came to Elisha, he said to her, "Pick up your son."

She bowed low to the ground before Elisha. Then she picked up her son and left the room.

Jonah and the Whale

The Book of Jonah 1–4

God spoke to Jonah, saying, "Go to the great city of Nineveh and proclaim its doom, for I have seen how wicked its people are."

But Jonah set out to run away from God. He went down to the harbor and found a ship there going in the opposite direction from Nineveh. He paid for his journey and went aboard.

Then God stirred up a strong wind that churned the sea into a violent storm, so that the ship was in danger of sinking. Terrified, the sailors cried out to their gods and threw the ship's cargo overboard to lighten the load. Jonah, meanwhile, went down into the hold of the ship and fell asleep.

The captain called to Jonah, "How can you sleep! Get up and call upon your god! Perhaps your god will take pity on us so that we will not die."

The sailors said to each other, "Let's cast lots to find out who's responsible for this evil that has come upon us."

So they cast lots, and the lot fell upon Jonah.

They asked him, "Tell us, you who have brought this evil upon us, what is your business? Where have you come from? What is your country, and who are your people?"

Jonah replied, "I am a Hebrew, and I worship the God of heaven who made the sea and the dry land."

The men were very frightened. They asked, "What have you done?"

When they learned that Jonah was running away from God, they said, "What must we do to you to calm the sea?" For the sea was growing wilder.

Jonah said, "Throw me overboard into the sea, and then it will become calm, for now I know that it is my fault that this great storm has come upon us."

The men tried to row the ship toward shore, but they made no headway, for the storm grew ever fiercer. So they cried out to God, "Please, God, do not let us die because of this man. Do not hold us guilty of spilling innocent blood! For it is you, O God, Who have caused all this to happen."

Then they lifted up Jonah and threw him overboard into the sea. And the sea became calm.

Then God sent a great fish to swallow Jonah. And he remained in the belly of the fish for three days and three nights.

Jonah prayed to God from the belly of the fish:

In my trouble I called to You,
And You answered me.
You flung me into the deep,
Into the heart of the sea.
Weeds twined around my head.
But You brought me up from the pit.
When my life was draining away,
I remembered God,
And my prayer came to You.

Then God spoke to the fish, and it spit Jonah out upon dry land.

God spoke to Jonah a second time, saying, "Go to the great city of Nineveh, and say what I tell you to say."

So Jonah went to Nineveh as God had commanded him.

Now Nineveh was an enormous city, a three-day walk from one end of the city to the other. Jonah walked through the city for one whole day, declaring, "In 40 days, Nineveh will be overthrown!"

Then the people of Nineveh believed in God. They declared a fast and dressed in mourning clothes, young and old alike. When word reached the king of Nineveh, he got up from his throne and took off his royal robes. He too dressed in coarse mourning cloth and sat down in the ashes.

Then he issued a decree that was announced throughout Nineveh: "By order of the king, every person and animal in Nineveh must fast. You must dress in rough cloth and cry out to God. Let each person turn back from doing evil and acting unjustly. Perhaps God will then turn back from destroying our city."

When God saw that the people of Nineveh were truly turning back from their evil ways, God decided not to punish them.

But Jonah was very angry about God's decision.

He prayed to God, "I knew this would happen even before I ran from You. And that is why I tried to flee. For I know that You are a compassionate and merciful God, slow to anger and full of kindness, and that You would decide not to punish the people of Nineveh. Please, God, take my life, for it is better for me to die than to live!"

God asked, "And why should you be so upset?"

Jonah then went out of Nineveh until he came to a place to the east of the city. There he built a booth and rested in its shade, waiting to see what would happen to Nineveh.

God provided a gourd plant that grew up over Jonah, sheltering him from wind and sun. Jonah was delighted with the gourd.

But early the next morning God sent a worm that attacked the gourd so that it shriveled up. When the sun rose, God sent a hot east wind. The sun beat down upon Jonah's head, and he became so faint that he wished to die.

He said, "It is better for me to die than to live!"

God asked, "Are you so upset about the gourd?"

Jonah replied, "Yes, so much so that I would rather die!"

God said, "You care about the gourd, which you neither grew nor tended, which sprang up and perished overnight. Should I not care about the great city of Nineveh, home to more than one hundred twenty thousand people who do not know their right hand from their left, as well as many animals?"

Ruth and Naomi

The Book of Ruth 1–4

In the days of the judges, there was once a famine in the land of Judah. And Elimelech and his wife, Naomi, and their two sons, left their home in Bethlehem and went to live in the land of Moab.

Elimelech died, and Naomi was left with her two sons. They married two Moabite women, Ruth and Orpah. But after 10 years, Naomi's sons also died, and Naomi was left without either husband or sons.

Then Naomi heard that the famine had ended in Judah. So she set off with her two daughters-in-law to return home.

But as they started on the road to Judah, Naomi said to Ruth and Orpah, "Turn back and go home to your families. May God be kind to you, as you have been kind to me and my family. And may God help you find new husbands."

Then she kissed them both good-bye.

Weeping, they said to her, "No, we'll return with you to your people."

Naomi replied, "Turn back, my daughters! Why should you go with me? Do I have more sons for you to marry?"

The two women wept again. Then Orpah kissed Naomi good-bye and headed back to Moab. But Ruth held on to her mother-in-law and would not let her go.

Naomi said, "See, your sister-in-law has returned to her people and her gods. Go with her."

Ruth replied, "Do not tell me to turn back and leave you. For wherever you go, I will go. Wherever you stay, I will stay. Your people will be my people, and your God will be my God. Wherever you die, there will I die, and there will I be buried. Only death will part us."

When Naomi saw that Ruth's mind was made up, she stopped arguing with her. And the two women walked on to Bethlehem. When they arrived, the whole city buzzed with excitement over their return.

The women of the city asked each other, "Can this be Naomi?"

Naomi said, "Do not call me Naomi, which means 'pleasant.' Instead call me Mara, which means 'bitter,' for God has made my life very bitter. I went away full and came back empty."

When Ruth and Naomi first arrived from Moab, it was the time of the barley harvest. In Bethlehem, Naomi had a relative on her husband's side, Boaz, who was a very wealthy man.

Not long after their return, Ruth said to her mother-in-law, "I would like to go to the barley fields to glean, to pick up the sheaves that fall from the reapers' hands."

Naomi said, "Yes, my daughter, go."

It happened that Ruth went to glean in a field owned by Boaz, the wealthy kinsman from Elimelech's family.

While she was working in his field, Boaz arrived from the city.

His eyes fell upon Ruth.

"Whose girl is that?" he asked the servant in charge of the reapers.

The servant replied, "She is a Moabite girl who came back with Naomi from the land of Moab. She asked to glean behind the reapers. She's been on her feet since morning, only stopping a little while to rest in the shade."

Boaz came up to Ruth and said to her, "Listen to me. Do not go to glean in another field, but stay here close to my women. Keep your eyes on the field and follow the women as they reap. I have ordered my men not to lay hands on you. And whenever you are thirsty, go drink some of the water that my men have drawn."

Ruth bowed low to the ground. "Why are you so kind to me? I am a foreigner here!"

Boaz replied, "I have heard how kind you were to your mother-in-law, Naomi, after her husband died, how you left your father and mother and the land where you were born to come to a land and a people you do not know. May the God of Israel, under whose wings you have come to shelter, grant you the reward you deserve!"

Ruth said, "You are most kind, my lord, to comfort me and to say such gentle words to me, even though I am not even your servant."

When it was mealtime, Boaz said to Ruth, "Come and have something to eat."

So she sat down among the reapers and ate the roasted grain Boaz gave her until she was full. When she went back to glean, Boaz said to his workers, "Drop extra stalks of barley for her and do not speak harshly to her as she works."

Ruth gleaned in the field until evening. Then she beat the stalks that she had gathered in order to separate the grains from the straw and carried the winnowed barley home to Naomi.

When Naomi saw how much grain Ruth had brought home, even after having eaten a portion as her day's meal, she asked her daughter-in-law, "Where did you work today? Blessed be the man who paid so much attention to you!"

Ruth replied, "I worked in the field of a man named Boaz."

Naomi cried, "Blessed be God! Boaz is our kinsman who can buy back our family's land."

Ruth said, "He told me to stay in his field until the harvest was finished."

"Then do so, my daughter."

So Ruth gleaned alongside Boaz's maidservants until the barley and wheat harvests were finished. Then she stayed home with Naomi.

After a time, Naomi said to her, "Ruth, I must find a home for you, where you will be happy. Go tonight to the threshing floor, where Boaz will be winnowing barley. Before you go, bathe, put on sweet-smelling oil, dress yourself up, and go to him, but do not show yourself to him until he has finished eating and drinking. Then go to where he is lying down, uncover his feet, and lie down next to him. He will then tell you what to do."

Ruth replied, "I will do everything you've told me."

So Ruth went to the threshing floor and did just as her mother-in-law had told her. Boaz ate and drank. Then in good spirits, he lay down beside the grainpile. Ruth crept over to him, uncovered his feet, and lay down. In the middle of the night, Boaz woke up. How startled he was to find a woman lying at his feet!

He asked, "Who are you?"

The woman replied, "I am your servant Ruth. I ask that you become my husband, so that you can redeem our family's land."

Boaz cried, "God bless you, Ruth! Your latest act of devotion is even greater than your first. For you could have looked for a younger husband, rich or poor, but you have not done so. Do not be afraid, Ruth. I will do whatever you ask. All the elders of the town know what a fine woman you are. But you should know that Naomi has another kinsman who is even more closely related to your family than I am. If he wishes to marry you—so be it. Let him buy back the family land. But if he does not wish to, I will gladly do so myself. Now lie down and stay here until morning."

Ruth lay down at Boaz's feet until dawn. She got up before it was light, for Boaz feared that word would spread that a woman had stayed with him all night on the threshing floor.

Boaz said to her, "Hold out your shawl." She held it out while he measured into it six measures of barley. He then put the bundle on her back.

Ruth went back to Naomi and told her everything that had happened.

Naomi said, "Stay here with me, my daughter, until you see how things turn out. Boaz will certainly make sure that the matter is settled today."

Boaz went to the town gate and sat down to wait. Soon Naomi's other close kinsman came by.

Boaz called to him, "Come over here and sit down."

The man sat down next to Boaz. Boaz then summoned ten elders of the town and asked them to sit at the gate as well.

Boaz said to the other kinsman, "Naomi has come back from Moab and must sell a piece of land belonging to her dead husband, Elimelech. Since you are a closer relative, you have first rights to buy back the land. If you are willing to do so, then do so. But if not, tell me, because I am next in line after you."

The man replied, "I am willing to buy it."

Then Boaz said, "When you buy this property from Naomi, you must also marry Ruth, the widow of Naomi's dead son, so you can carry on the family name."

The man replied, "That I cannot do, because then my inheritance would go to Elimelekh's family, not my own. So I now turn over to you my right as closest kinsman."

Boaz said to the elders and the rest of the people, "Today you are all witnesses that I am buying from Naomi all the land that once belonged to Elimelekh and their two sons. I am also marrying Ruth, to carry on the family name."

All the people replied, "We are witnesses! May God make the woman coming into your house like Rachel and Leah, who built up the House of Israel. May your name become famous in Bethlehem. May you and this young woman have children to carry on your name!"

So Boaz married Ruth, and they had a son.

The women said to Naomi, "Your grandson will renew your life and care for you in your old age. For he is born to your daughter-in-law Ruth, who loves you and is kinder to you than seven sons."

Naomi picked up the child and held him close to her. She became like another mother to him.

They named the boy Obed. He was the grandfather of King David.

Esther Saves Her People

The Book of Esther 1–10

In the third year of his reign, King Ahasuerus, who ruled over 127 provinces from India to Ethiopia, gave a banquet in the Persian capital of Shushan, inviting all the officials, nobles, and governors of his realm. For 180 days, the king showed off the tremendous riches of his kingdom. Then he held a special banquet in the palace garden for everyone who lived in Shushan. And the king gave orders: "No limits on wine!"

Elsewhere in the palace, Queen Vashti gave a separate banquet for the women.

After seven days of feasting, when the king was tipsy with wine, he ordered his seven chamberlains to bring out Queen Vashti dressed in her royal crown, to show off her great beauty to the king and his guests.

But Queen Vashti refused to appear, and Ahasuerus was furious.

The king asked his advisers, "What shall be done, according to law, to Queen Vashti for disobeying the king's command?"

The king's advisers replied, "The queen has offended not only Your majesty but all the officials and all the peoples throughout your kingdom. The queen's behavior will make all wives disobey their husbands. All the women of Persia will follow her example! Therefore, let the king banish Vashti from Your Majesty's presence and choose another to take her place. This way, all wives, high and low, will treat their husbands with respect."

The proposal pleased the king. So messengers were sent throughout the kingdom, announcing that every man should rule in his own home.

Then the king commanded that all beautiful young single women in his kingdom be brought to the palace and handed over to the guardian of the harem.

Now there lived in Shushan a Jew named Mordecai, whose family had long ago been exiled from Jerusalem. He was foster father to his cousin Esther, who was also known as Hadassah, whom he had adopted when her parents died.

The beautiful young Esther was brought to the royal harem along with many other young women. The king favored her and treated her with special kindness. Mordecai advised Esther not to reveal her identity to anyone, so she told no one that she was a Jew. Every day, Mordecai would walk near the rooms of the harem to see how Esther was doing.

For the next 12 months, all the young women who had been brought to the harem were pampered with oils, perfumes, and cosmetics. Then, one by one, they were brought before the king. When it was Esther's turn, she pleased Ahasuerus more than all the others. So he set a royal crown upon her head and made her queen in place of Vashti. To celebrate, he held a special banquet in her honor, canceled all taxes, and gave out gifts throughout his kingdom.

But Esther still did not reveal her true identity, as Mordecai had instructed her.

One day, when Mordecai was sitting at the palace gate, he overheard two of the king's chamberlains plotting to assassinate the king. Mordecai reported the plot to Queen Esther, who told the king what Mordecai had discovered. The matter was investigated and found to be true. The two plotters were put to death. And the whole matter was written down in the royal Book of Records.

Some time after this, King Ahasuerus promoted Haman to be chief of his court officials. All the other officials bowed down before him, as the king had commanded—except for Mordecai, who refused to kneel or bow.

They said to Mordecai, "Why do you disobey the king's command?"

Mordecai replied, "As a Jew, I cannot bow to Haman."

When Haman saw for himself that Mordecai would not kneel or bow before him, he was furious. He made up his mind to punish not only

Mordecai but all the Jews in Ahasuerus's kingdom. To choose when Haman would take his revenge, they cast lots—*purim*. The lot fell on Adar, the 12th month of the year.

Haman then came before King Ahasuerus and said, "There is a certain people, scattered across your kingdom whose laws are different from those of any other people. They do not obey the king's laws. It is not in Your Majesty's interest to put up with them. Therefore, let the king give orders to destroy them. And I will personally contribute ten thousand pieces of silver to your royal treasury."

The king gave his signet ring to Haman and said, "Do as you see fit."

And so a royal decree was issued and sealed with the king's ring: On the 13th day of the month of Adar, all the Jews in Ahasuerus's kingdom—young and old, men, women, and children—were to be killed, and their possessions seized.

At once messengers were sent to every province to announce this decree. Then the king and Haman sat down to celebrate. But the city of Shushan was astounded.

When Mordecai learned about the king's decree, he tore his clothing and put on coarse cloth and ashes. And throughout the kingdom, the Jews fasted, wept, and mourned, dressing themselves in coarse mourning cloth and ashes.

When Esther's maids told her about the king's decree, she was very distressed. She sent one of her servants to speak to Mordecai, who told the servant all that had happened and sent back to Esther a copy of the royal decree. He also sent instructions that Esther should appear before the king to plead for her people's lives.

Esther sent back her reply to Mordecai: "Anyone who approaches the king's throne without being summoned to appear is put to death. Only if the king extends his golden scepter will that person's life be spared. But I have not been summoned for the last 30 days."

Mordecai sent a message back to Esther: "Do not think that you will be the only Jew to escape death, just because you live in the king's palace. No, if you keep silent, help will come to the Jews from another place, and you and your family will be lost. Who knows, maybe you have become queen for just such a crisis as this."

Esther sent back her reply: "Gather together all the Jews of Shushan and have them fast on my behalf. For three days and nights, let none of them eat or drink. My maids and I will observe the same fast. Then I will go before the king, even though it means breaking the law. And if I am to die, then I will die!"

And Mordecai did as Esther had commanded him.

Three days later, Esther dressed in her royal robes and stood outside the throne room, where the king sat upon his throne. As soon as the king saw her, he held out his golden scepter to her.

The king asked, "What troubles you, Queen Esther? What is your wish? Even if you ask for half of my kingdom, it shall be yours."

Esther replied, "If it please Your Majesty, let Your Highness and Haman come today to a feast I have prepared."

The king commanded, "Tell Haman to hurry and do the queen's bidding."

That night both men came to the feast that Esther had prepared.

As they sat eating and drinking, the king asked Esther again, "What is your wish? Even if you ask for half of my kingdom, it is yours."

Esther replied, "Let Your Highness and Haman come to another feast I will prepare for them."

Haman left the palace happy. But when he saw Mordecai sitting in the palace gate, not getting up as Haman passed by, he was furious. But he controlled himself and went on his way.

When Haman came home, he told his wife Zeresh and his friends about his good fortune, especially about the feast the queen had made for him and the second feast she was preparing for the following day.

He told them, "But all this means nothing to me when I see that Jew Mordecai!"

Zeresh and his friends advised him, "Erect a tall wooden stake, and tomorrow ask the king to impale Mordecai upon it. Then you can go to the feast with a glad heart."

Their proposal pleased Haman, and he had the stake erected.

That night the king could not sleep. He ordered his attendant to read to him from the royal Book of Records to him. It so happened that the part the servant read concerned the assassination plot against the king that Mordecai had discovered and exposed.

The king asked, "What honor was done for this Mordecai?"

His servant replied, "Nothing at all."

The king asked, "Who is waiting in the outer court?"

It so happened that Haman had just entered the outer court to ask the king to impale Mordecai on the stake he had erected for him.

The servant replied, "Haman is standing in the court."

The king commanded, "Let him enter."

So Haman came before the king.

The king asked him, "What should be done to the man the king wishes to honor?"

Thinking that the king meant him, Haman replied, "Let him be dressed in the king's robes and crowned with the king's crown, be seated upon the king's horse, and be paraded through the city by a court official, crying, 'This is what is done for the man the king wishes to honor.'"

The king said, "Quick, then! Get my robes and horse, and do all this to Mordecai the Jew, who sits in the palace gate."

So Haman dressed Mordecai in royal robes and crowned him, and paraded him through the city, proclaiming, "This is what is done for the man the king wishes to honor!"

When he was done, Haman hurried home, his head hung in shame. When he told Zeresh and his friends what had happened, they said to him,

"If you have already begun to fall before Mordecai the Jew, you're surely doomed."

Just then, the king's attendant arrived to summon Haman to Esther's banquet.

At the feast, the king again asked Esther, "What is your wish? Even if you ask for half of my kingdom, it is yours."

The queen replied, "My wish is that my life be spared and also the lives of my people. For my people and I have been betrayed, singled out to be murdered."

"Who dares to do this?" demanded the king.

Esther replied, "Here is the enemy—this evil Haman!"

Haman cringed in terror before the king and queen. Furious, the king stormed out into the palace garden. Haman fell face down on Esther's couch to plead for his life.

When the king came back into the room, he found Haman lying on Esther's couch, beside the queen.

The king cried, "So, he even dares to assault the queen in my own palace!"

One of the king's attendants added, "What is more, Haman has built a stake on which to impale Mordecai, whose words once saved the king's life."

The king ordered, "Impale Haman on it instead!"

And so they impaled Haman upon the stake meant for Mordecai. Only then did the king's anger cool.

That day, King Ahasuerus gave Haman's property to Queen Esther. When Esther revealed to the king that Mordecai was her cousin, Ahasuerus gave Mordecai his signet ring, which he had taken back from Haman. And Esther put Mordecai in charge of Haman's property.

Then Esther fell down before the king, weeping and pleading with him to prevent the evil plot against the Jews that Haman had set into motion.

She said to him, "Let the king send messengers throughout the kingdom canceling Haman's decree to kill the Jews. How can I stand by and witness the destruction of my own people!"

The king said to Esther and Mordecai, "I have already executed Haman and have given you his property. But I cannot cancel the decree. For whatever has been decreed in the king's name and sealed with the king's seal cannot be reversed. You must write your own decree concerning the Jews, ordering it in my name and sealing it with my seal."

So Mordecai dictated letters in the king's name and sealed them with the king's seal. Messengers then rode forth on swift royal steeds, carrying the letters to all 127 provinces from India to Ethiopia. The decree was addressed to the Jews in their own language and writing, and to every other people in their own language and writing. The decree proclaimed: "The king permits Jews in every city and in the capital city of Shushan to gather together and fight for their lives!"

Then Mordecai left the king's presence wearing a golden crown, royal robes of blue and white, and a cape made of fine linen and purple wool.

On that day, the city of Shushan rejoiced. Throughout the realm, the Jews enjoyed light and gladness, happiness and honor. Everywhere, there was feasting and celebration. And on the 13th day of Adar, when the Jews had been condemned to die, just the opposite happened: Throughout the kingdom, Jews defended themselves against their attackers and were victorious.

The next day, they celebrated a holiday, eating and drinking and making merry.

Mordecai and Queen Esther decreed that every year on this day, Jews throughout the kingdom were to celebrate the holiday of Purim with feasting and joy, sending gifts to one another and to the poor. And Esther's decree about the holiday of Purim was recorded in a scroll.

Daniel in the Lions' Den

Daniel 1–2; 5:30–6:29

Among the Jewish exiles that King Nebuchadnezzar brought to Babylon were several handsome young men of noble birth, learned and wise. Nebuchadnezzar ordered them to be taught the Babylonian language, to be fed from the royal kitchens, and to be schooled for three years. Then they were to enter the king's service.

Among these men was Daniel, who was given the Babylonian name Belteshazzar. Daniel was talented in interpreting dreams and was appointed to a position of great power and authority by King Nebuchadnezzar and by his son Belshazzar who ruled after him.

Then Belshazzar was killed, and Darius became king. Darius appointed Daniel and two other ministers to rule over the 120 governors in charge of the kingdom, but Daniel possessed such an extraordinary spirit that Darius placed him in charge of all the ministers and governors in the kingdom.

The other ministers and governors wanted to disgrace Daniel, but they could not find any fault with him, for he was trustworthy and honest. So they said, "We will not be able to disgrace him unless we can find something against him that has to do with the laws of his God."

They went to the king and said, "All the ministers and governors in your kingdom have decided that you should issue a royal decree making it a crime to make a plea to anyone, human or divine, besides you. And you should further order that anyone who disobeys this law during the next 30 days will be punished by being thrown into the lions' den. Put this decree in writing, O king, so no one can reverse it."

When Daniel heard of the decree, he went to the upper room of his house, where he had had windows made to face Jerusalem. As was his practice three times each day, he knelt down, prayed, and confessed to God.

At that moment, the plotters came into the room and found Daniel making a plea to his God.

They went and told the king: "Did you not just issue a decree making it illegal for your subjects to make a plea to anyone besides you, O king, over the next 30 days?"

The king replied, "Indeed, the decree stands as a law and may not be canceled."

They said, "Daniel, one of the exiles of Judah, has disobeyed your law. Three times each day he makes pleas to his God."

When Darius heard this, he was very distressed. He wished to save Daniel, using every means available to him. But when the sun set, the plotters returned to Darius and said, "O king, it is the law that a royal decree cannot be changed."

So with a heavy heart, the king ordered Daniel thrown into the lions' den. He said to Daniel, "The God whom you serve so faithfully will surely save you."

Then an immense rock was rolled over the mouth of the den, sealing Daniel inside with the lions. The king sealed the den with his signet ring so that nothing could be changed concerning Daniel's fate.

Then the king went to his palace and fasted all night. He refused all amusements and was unable to sleep. At the first light of dawn, he rushed to the lions' den. Approaching the rock sealing off the entrance, he cried out in a voice filled with sorrow, "Daniel, servant of the living God, has the God you serve so faithfully saved you from the lions?"

Daniel replied from within the lions' den, "My God sent an angel who closed up the lions' mouths so that they did not harm me. For I have done nothing wrong before my God or my king."

Darius rejoiced when he heard these words, and he ordered that Daniel be released immediately from the lions' den. When they looked him over, they found not one scratch on him, for he had trusted in God.

Then King Darius issued a new decree addressed to all people, written in every language on earth: "Peace be with you! I hereby order that all my subjects within my royal domain must honor the God of Daniel, the God who lives forever, whose kingdom lasts until the end of time. God performs miracles and wonders in heaven and on earth. For God saved Daniel from the jaws of lions."

Writing a Jewish Children's Bible:
An Author's Notebook

My chief aim in writing this book has been to introduce American children to the language and rhythms of the Hebrew Bible. These stories have been adapted from the 1985 JPS Translation (known also as NJPS, or the New JPS Translation). Over a 30-year period (1955–85), three teams of JPS translators sought to render the ancient Hebrew masoretic text as faithfully as possible, in contrast to their predecessors whose 1917 English translation, published as *The Holy Scriptures* (also known as OJPS), did not differ greatly from the 17th-century classic King James Version (KJV), except that the JPS translation eliminated anti-Jewish and Christological language.

Unlike KJV, OJPS, and many other English translations, the language of NJPS is colloquial, fluid, almost contemporary in its cadences. All archaisms—thee and thou, slayest, and begat—are gone, and the tenor of the prose tends toward the informal and idiomatic. Although some have objected to this "dressing down" of sacred writ, there is no doubt that the narrative portions have greatly benefited from this colloquial approach. That is why the stories in this book always begin with the NJPS text.

But even an idiomatic translation needs some adjustment to accommodate young American readers in the early 21st century. Following are explanations and examples, divided into categories, of the instances where I depart from the 1985 JPS Translation.

—~— ❋ —~—

Diction

A translator's job is to choose words in a second language that correspond as closely as possible to the word choices of the original author. A skillful translator will also seek to convey nuances beyond a word's denotation (its dictionary meaning). Such nuances include wordplay (such as puns and double entendres), etymology, irony, allusion, alliteration, and near rhyme and levels of social status as revealed in dialogue. When adapting a translation for children, an author also has to consider her audience's reading proficiency, vocabulary, cultural literacy, and maturity.

Here are a few examples:

- ※ Unfamiliar vocabulary. The Hebrew Bible was written for adults. Even in English translation, there are many words that are unfamiliar to American children. In these cases, I have substituted familiar vocabulary. However, I made an exception in cases when a different form of an unfamiliar word remains current in our everyday speech. So, for example, though modern children might be unaccustomed to hearing the word "conceive" used to mean "become pregnant," they probably have heard of "contraceptives," "something used to prevent conceiving." Similarly, although they might not recognize the verb "to abstain," they have probably learned about abstentions in the voting process. It's useful for children to learn that the root of an English word can take multiple forms, just as is the case with the *shoresh* in the Hebrew language.

- ※ No contemporary equivalents. Some terms in Hebrew have no contemporary equivalents in English, because the social or religious institutions they describe have ceased to exist. That's why I've retained some archaic words like "viceroy" and "concubine"; no modern terms correspond to these ancient social roles. However, following the example of other translations, I have rendered the word "*sarees*" (used throughout the Book of Esther) as "chamberlain" instead of "eunuch," since the latter term may distress some parents and children.

- ※ Changes in connotation. Sometimes an English word no longer means what it once did in the time of King James I or even of Queen Victoria. So, for example, the word, "fear," which once meant to "stand in awe of," has lost that connotation in contemporary English. For that reason, I have chosen to translate the Hebrew "*yirah*" as "fear and respect" in order to convey both senses that the word once carried in English usage.

- ※ The special diction of Scripture. I want to give children a feel for the special diction that characterizes sacred texts. These texts generally exclude street language and slang as well as trendy idioms. Though the colloquialism of NJPS makes the Bible very accessible to modern readers, it sometimes veers too close to everyday language. To sharpen the difference between the sacred and the everyday, I occasionally choose a less familiar synonym for a certain word. So, for example, in place of "run away" (NJPS), I substitute the less common "flee"; for "caught up with" (NJPS), the less common "overtook." I also limit the use of contractions, avoiding them in dialogue in which God or angels speak and using them sparingly in the speech of leaders and kings. Exceptions generally occur when someone of high rank speaks to someone of lesser rank, such as monarch to commoner, or master to servant. Contractions do not appear in straight narration.

※ "To know" in the biblical sense. One awkward issue to resolve in a children's Bible is how to translate the Hebrew word, "*yadah,*" which means both "to know" something and "to know" someone sexually. (Though the second meaning has become obsolete in contemporary English, most adults nonetheless still chuckle when someone refers to "knowing 'in the biblical sense.'") In most cases, I translate "*yadah*" as "became pregnant," thereby shifting the focus from the sexual act to its result. However, in the story of Sodom and Gomorrah, that strategy does not work since it is men, not women, whom the evil Sodomites wish to violate. When they demand that Lot bring out his two male houseguests, "that we may *yadah* them," I've translated the word as "lay hands on" to suggest both sexual desire and violence (in contrast to the milder "be intimate with" of NJPS).

※ Funny modern connotations. Some common words, such as "kid," meaning "young goat," have become double entendres in modern colloquial English. That's why young children titter when the Bible speaks of sacrificing kids. To avoid these titters, I've substituted "young goat" for "kid." Similarly, certain words, such as "rod," "ass," and "bosom," carry sexual connotations in modern English, which may embarrass some young readers. I have substituted synonyms for them as well.

Translation

Despite the many virtues of the JPS Translation, there are certain instances when I opt for a different translation or choose to use my own. These instances include cases in which (1) a story works better for children when a narrative section is condensed or summarized; (2) the NJPS is too obscure, abstract, or sophisticated for young children to understand; (3) the more formal language of OJPS seems better suited to the subject matter than the idiomatic language of NJPS; or (4) I disagree with NJPS.

Here are some examples:

※ *Ketonet passim*. NJPS translates "*ketonet passim,*" the coat that Jacob gives to Joseph, as an "ornamented tunic" (Gen 37:3). But the NJPS translator adds a footnote that reads: "or 'a coat of many colors'; meaning of Heb.

uncertain." I've chosen to use the wording in the translator's note, "coat of many colors," because this phrase is both more familiar and more concrete.

※ *Bamah* vs. *mizbe'ah.* Much of the Bible's technical vocabulary concerning priestly and levitical clothing, furniture, architecture, ritual implements, and the like makes no sense to children. Therefore, I've chosen to conflate some of the Bible's fine distinctions so as not to confuse young readers. So, for example, though the Bible uses two different Hebrew terms to refer to altars—"*bamah*" to refer to local Israelite altars, and "*mizbe'ah,*" for the altar in the Jerusalem Temple—I have not followed NJPS in using two different English words, "shrine" and "altar," respectively, but have instead used "altar" to refer to both.

※ The Name of God. For the most part, I use the word "God" whenever the Hebrew text refers to the Divine. However, in a few cases—the Burning Bush, Moses and Aaron's appearances before Pharaoh, the contest between Elijah and the priests of Baal—I use instead YHVH, the transliterated Four-Letter Divine Name (known also as the Tetragrammaton). Although children won't know how to read this transliterated word (which was never meant to be pronounced except by the High Priest) and won't know what these four letters represent, I encourage parents and teachers to learn more from a knowledgeable person or a reliable source about how Jewish tradition has historically related to God's name.

Hebrew

I would have liked to include many Hebrew words in transliterated form so that English-speaking children could become accustomed to the sounds of biblical language, but I was ultimately persuaded that transliteration is simply too confusing for most children. Even with transliteration, it is almost impossible to translate Hebrew wordplay and allusion into English. I therefore limit transliteration to those instances in which knowing the Hebrew word is key to understanding a particular story or character.

Here are some examples:

※ Repetition. One of the ways that the Bible draws implicit connections between personalities and stories is by repeating the same Hebrew word in two or more stories. So, for example, the root "*yrh,*" meaning "to see," is a leitmotif in the Genesis stories concerning Abraham and Hagar. Similarly, an identical Hebrew phrase, *yefat to'ar ve-yefat mar'eh,* is used to describe

Rachel and, in a later narrative, her elder son, Joseph. (I owe this insight to a note by Everett Fox in his Schocken Bible translation.) To draw these parallels, I use the identical English phrase, "graceful and fair," to describe both Rachel and Joseph, hoping that readers will thereby connect Jacob's favoritism toward his wife Rachel and his similar favoritism toward Rachel's firstborn son, Joseph.

※ Etymology of names. The Bible usually provides etymologies to explain the names of significant characters (for the most part, only males). So, for example, Isaac's Hebrew name, *Yitzhak*, means "to laugh" (which is what his mother Sarah does when she is told she will bear a child in old age). It also means to mock. To conjure up both meanings of *ZHK*, the Hebrew root of Isaac's name, I've translated this word when it describes Ishmael's behavior in Genesis 21:9 as "clowning around" as opposed to the more neutral "playing" in NJPS.

※ And. A great number of biblical verses begin with the Hebrew letter *vav*, which can be translated as "and," "but," or "then." This prefix also performs a grammatical function, reversing the tense of the verb to which it is attached. Unlike English sentences, which rarely begin with "and," biblical narratives are by and large stitched together by these initial *vav*'s. By choosing to begin many of my sentences with "and," I hope to attune children's ears to the traditional rhythm of biblical storytelling.

Editing

I have tried not to get in the Bible's way. When I do, it is only because I want to be helpful to my young readers.

Here are some examples:

※ Redundancies. Some stories, such as Eliezer's mission to find a bride for Isaac ("Rebekah at the Well"), include the same account told and retold. I've eliminated such retellings when they don't advance the plot or build suspense. However, I've kept double or even triple tellings in cases in which they satisfy the conventions of storytelling, which children intuitively understand. Such is the case in the story of Balaam.

※ Added words. On rare occasions, I insert an extra word or phrase into a story or substitute my own words in order to ensure that a narrative makes sense. So, for example, in the Joseph story, the Bible twice refers to Jacob as

"Israel." In both instances, I've changed "Israel" to "Jacob" so that young readers will realize that it is the same person.

Commentary

As I've said, I want the Bible to speak for itself. My interpretations and commentary do not belong in this book. However, the Bible is an ancient document, which has lost some clarity over the millennia. In order to sharpen its sound so that it speaks clearly to the children of the 21st century, I have made a few editorial interventions, which I hope are both helpful and unobtrusive.

Here is an example:

※ Explanatory phrase, word, or bracketed addition. Sometimes adding a word can help readers visualize an object, place, or concept that they would not otherwise understand. So, for example, in the story of Joseph and his brothers, I expand the word "pit" (NJPS) to "water pit" (a desert cistern), which is a reservoir hollowed out of stone. Simply substituting the word "cistern" for "pit" would not have been helpful since most American children don't know what a cistern is. Similarly, "sackcloth" is incomprehensible to children today, so I translated it as "coarse mourning cloth," a more vivid description of the animal-skin or hemp material used as sacking in the ancient Near East and also donned by mourners.

Objectionable or Adult Material

One of the hardest challenges facing the author of a children's Bible is what to do with material considered by parents, teachers, or other authority figures as too adult. I had to make some tough judgment calls about protecting the sensibilities of young children while at the same time accurately representing the harsh realities and lessons of the Bible.

I was guided here by some of my young readers themselves as well as by my colleagues at JPS. Several preteens who read a draft of the manuscript objected to the violence and sex in some of the stories. Because of this feedback, I decided to exclude "The Rape of Dinah"—despite its later echoes in Jacob's blessing and in Moses' final speech, as well as its homiletic value as an object lesson. I also chose to exclude the disturbing story, "Jephthah's Daughter." In several included stories, I eliminated certain passages that contain overly graphic violence or sex.

However, there are certain problematic stories that I've left in, largely unexpurgated, such as "The Binding of Isaac" and the story of "David and Bathsheba." These stories will undoubtedly challenge a young person's sensibilities and sense of justice. But such is the legacy of Jewish history and legend and the source of the Jewish literary and legal traditions. Rather than censor all such difficult material (as has been done for centuries in most children's Bibles), I hope that parents, teachers, and rabbis will talk with young readers about these stories and will encourage them to continue wrestling with these difficult texts throughout their lives—with the help of classical rabbinic commentaries, modern scholarship, members of their communities, and their own conscience. I have also included some scenes of graphic violence, especially in the Book of Judges, because their moral consequences still resonate with us today.

Gender

The Bible emerged out of a culture radically different from our own. The roles played by men and women in that ancient time and place bear little resemblance to gender roles today. To be fair to the Bible, we cannot impose our contemporary values of feminism and gender equality upon it. But to be fair to ourselves, we cannot simply sweep aside the contradictions between the Bible's world and our own. The way that I address this challenge is to represent God as gender-neutral, following the tradition of Maimonides, who cautioned us not to characterize the divine in human terms. I also honor the sympathy of the ancient Rabbis, who invented names for the nameless women of the Bible, filled in their fragmentary biographies, and collapsed their own times and issues into the biblical chronicle.

Here are some examples:

  ※ Pronouns. Hebrew is a highly gendered language. Throughout the Bible, God is referred to as "He." Most English Bible translations to this day continue that practice. However, Judaism itself teaches, beginning with the Third Commandment, that God does not resemble earthly creatures, including human beings. In other words, God lacks a physical body and, therefore, has no gender. Unfortunately, human language does, and it is usually male. In this book, I eliminate all masculine pronouns with God as their antecedent. To do so requires that I sometimes repeat the word "God" too many times instead of using pronouns; other times I resort to passive voice. But I think that this stylistic awkwardness is worth it, because it encourages our children to stop thinking of God as an old bearded man seated on a throne.

  ※ The Name of God. Some feminist scholars argue that the word "lord" is exclusively male and should, therefore, not be used to refer to God. Others counter that "lord" is a generic term, suggesting authority and regency. My choice is to avoid its use altogether, substituting the word "God" whenever "Lord" appears in NJPS.

※ Women's names. The Bible is filled with nameless women. In some cases, a woman may be nameless in one part of a story but named in another. So, for instance, Miriam's name is not mentioned in the story of her brother Moses' birth but is simply referred to as "his sister." However, she is mentioned by name later on. I have chosen to use her name from the beginning of her family's story.

This is only a sampling of the choices I made when writing this book. My intent has always been to enhance the reading experience of the child. I hope that I've succeeded more often than not.

—·—※—·—

I would like to acknowledge the help of the many people who made this book possible. My interest in writing a children's Bible dates back to conversations I had almost 15 years ago with Chaim Potok z"l, my predecessor and mentor at JPS. His encouragement, together with that of Esther Hautzig, a longtime member of the JPS Editorial Committee and a dear friend, eventually led to my writing this volume.

It was wonderful working with my talented colleagues at JPS—Carol Hupping, Rena Potok, Janet Liss, Robin Norman, Michael Pomante, and Laurie Schlesinger— not as their boss but as a JPS author. From start to finish, my experience has been deeply gratifying. It has also been a pleasure to work with artist Avi Katz, whose enthusiasm for the project spurred him to draw many more illustrations than he had originally agreed to provide.

I want to thank as well the young volunteer reviewers who read the manuscript at an early stage and shared their feedback with me: Gina Vandetty, Eitana Friedman-Nathan, Naomi Esther Hollo, Eliana Actor-Engel, and Nisa Constantin-Raz. Their candid responses influenced my final selection of stories and reassured me that I was pitching the book at the appropriate level.

And as always, I owe much to Herbie for his ongoing support and counsel. Every book I've written bears his imprint.

The Books of the Hebrew Bible

THE TORAH

Genesis

The Creation of the World
Adam and Eve
The Serpent in the Garden
The First Murder
The Great Flood
The Tower of Babel
Abram and Sarai Leave Home
The Birth of Ishmael
Sarah Laughs
Sodom and Gomorrah
The Birth of Isaac
The Binding of Isaac
Rebekah at the Well
Jacob Steals the Birthright
Jacob's Dream
The Trickster Gets Tricked
Jacob Wrestles with an Angel
Joseph the Dreamer
From Slave to Viceroy
Joseph Tests His Brothers

Exodus

Pharaoh and the Hebrew Midwives
The Birth of Moses
Moses Flees to Midian
The Burning Bush
The Ten Plagues
The Splitting of the Sea of Reeds
The Gifts of Manna and Quail
The Ten Commandments
The Golden Calf

Leviticus

Numbers

The Twelve Spies
The Rebellion of Korah
Moses Strikes the Rock
Balaam and His Talking Donkey

Deuteronomy

Moses Says Good-Bye

THE PROPHETS

THE WRITINGS

Index